Work For The Brannans? Full-time?

She'd already decided she couldn't survive the few hours a week required to teach the boys etiquette—and their dad wanted her to *live* with them?

The look on Malinda's face was enough to let Jack know he was in trouble. But damn it, he and his boys needed her. Quickly, before she had a chance to refuse, he grabbed her hand. "Why don't you spend the rest of the day with us? Get to know us better?"

Brown eyes held Malinda's blue ones. She could tell that this man was dangerous. How could she possibly live in the same house with him when she couldn't even *breathe* when he stood this close?

She was crazy to even consider the idea. The Brannan boys were almost more than she could handle. And their father... he was *definitely* more than she could handle.

Dear Reader,

Happy holidays! At this busy time of year, I think it's extra important for you to take some time out for yourself. And what better way to get away from all the hustle and bustle of the season than to curl up somewhere with a Silhouette Desire novel? In addition, these books can make great gifts. Celebrate this season by giving the gift of love!

To get yourself in the holiday spirit, you should start with Lass Small's delightful *Man of the Month* book, *'Twas the Night*. Our hero has a plain name—Bob Brown—but as you fans of Lass Small all know, this will be no plain story. It's whimsical fun that only Lass can create.

The rest of December's lineup is equally wonderful. First, popular author Mary Lynn Baxter brings us a sexy, emotional love story, *Marriage, Diamond Style*. This is a book you'll want to keep. Next, Justine Davis makes her Silhouette Desire debut with *Angel for Hire*. The hero of this very special story is a *real* angel. The month is completed with stellar books by Jackie Merritt, Donna Carlisle and Peggy Moreland—winners all!

So go wild with Desire, and have a *wonderful* holiday season.

All the best,

Lucia Macro
Senior Editor

PEGGY MORELAND

MISS PRIM

SILHOUETTE *Desire*®

Published by Silhouette Books New York

America's Publisher of Contemporary Romance

SILHOUETTE BOOKS
300 East 42nd St., New York, N.Y. 10017

MISS PRIM

ISBN: 0-373-05682-6

First Silhouette Books printing December 1991

Printed in the U.S.A.

Books by Peggy Moreland

Silhouette Desire

A Little Bit Country #515
Run for the Roses #598
Miss Prim #682

PEGGY MORELAND,

a native Texan, has moved nine times in thirteen years of marriage. She has come to look at her husband's transfers as "extended vacations." Each relocation has required a change of career for Peggy: high school teacher, real-estate broker, accountant, antique-shop owner. Now the couple resides in Oklahoma with their three children, and Peggy is working on a master's degree in creative studies while doing what she loves best—writing!

For Paige, Hilary and Jess—
the inspiration behind all the "kids" in my stories
and the three little darlings who prove daily that
life is always stranger—and sometimes funnier—
than fiction.

One

Jack Brannan was as nervous as a whore in church. Surrounded by more froufrou than he'd encountered in a lifetime, he shoved his hands deep into his pockets and concentrated hard on not touching anything feminine or personal.

He'd never realized what an all-man world he lived in—until now. Pants that zipped up the front. Shirts that buttoned to the left. Commode lids constantly raised in the upright position. Loud voices, cussing and backslapping. Those were the things he was accustomed to. He glanced around the crowded store and suppressed a shudder.

A high-pitched squeal behind him made him jump, and he quickly sidestepped to avoid a collision with two little girls playing chase around a rack of dresses. The action proved to be a mistake—the first of many—for he immediately slammed into a woman weighed down with an armload of clothes.

Momentarily blinded by a cloud of satin and lace, he made a wild grab for the woman to keep her from falling . . . and filled his hands with soft, bare skin. Not certain what part of her anatomy he held, he quickly dropped his hands to his sides and watched helplessly as the bulk of the dresses fell to the floor.

His face burned in embarrassment. Mumbling an apology, he stooped to pick up the clothes—but was careful to touch only the plastic hangers' metal hooks.

The woman laughed easily at his discomfort. "Don't worry about it." She slipped the hangers she had managed to hold on to over the rack, then turned and took the dresses from him. She offered him an understanding smile. "It's always a madhouse when class is over. Are you here to pick up your daughter?"

"No." He glanced around the room crowded with giggling girls and gossiping mothers and suppressed another shudder. He was definitely out of his element. "I'm here to see Malinda Compton."

In response, the woman lifted one eyebrow. "Oh? Is she expecting you?"

He sucked in a deep breath and returned his hands to his jeans pockets and out of harm's way. "No." Already regretting the impulsive decision to seek Miss Compton's help, he turned to leave. "Maybe it'd be better if I came another time."

Before he could escape, the woman caught him by the arm. "I'm Cecile, Malinda's partner." She nodded toward the doorway to a side room where a woman stood, shaking hands with young girls as they filed by. "That's Malinda there. It looks as if she's almost through with her class."

Glancing in the direction Cecile indicated, Jack watched the woman smile as she clasped a little girl's small, white-gloved hand in hers. The child dropped a curtsy that would

val that offered a queen before she giggled and slipped out
ne door.

Oh, God, he thought, forgetting his earlier embarrassment and stifling a laugh, he could just *see* his kids' reac-
ons if he were to bring Miss Compton home.

Not that it was a hardship to look at her, he conceded as
e gave her a quick once-over. Yet he knew if he'd put
much thought into what "Miss Prim"—the author of the
Daily Oklahoman's etiquette column—would look like, he
would have painted an entirely different picture.

An old maid. That's what he would've expected. Draped
from neck to ankle in something dark and conservative and
wearing an expression like maybe she'd just taken a bite out
of a sour lemon. Instead he was confronted with a young
woman decked out in a sweater that looked as fluffy and
delectable as pink cotton candy. He ended his study at the
hem of her skirt, which was cut short enough to reveal well-
formed calves.

His one consolation was that, beyond the physical, his
expectations were right on target. Refined. That was the
first word that came to mind. Posture perfect and fully in
control of the situation. No baggy panty hose here, and not
a hair out of place. And starched, he thought, chuckling to
himself. She had enough starch in her spine to launder a
corporate executive's shirts for a month.

As the line of little girls exiting the room continued, he
wondered how she managed to hold the smile in place. Being locked up in the same room with twenty-five kids for
two hours couldn't be easy. Yet she handled it all with a
grace and a calmness that never wavered.

Nice smile, he noted, focusing on it. Friendly, encouraging. And the kids seemed to like her, he reflected as a cute
little blonde slipped her arms around Miss Compton's waist
for a quick hug. But *his* kids? No way!

"Why don't you wait in Malinda's office?" Cecile offered helpfully. "I'll tell her you're here."

Before he could decline the offer, Jack found himself herded toward the back of the store and settled in an overstuffed chair in the back office.

After placing a steaming mug of coffee in his hand, Cecile smiled and backed through the open doorway. "Just make yourself comfortable. Malinda shouldn't be more than a minute or two."

The door closed, muffling the voices and laughter from the store beyond. Jack's breath eased out of him on a slow sigh of relief. Carefully balancing the coffee mug on his knee, he glanced around the office. His fingers tightened convulsively on the mug.

If the store itself had made him uneasy, the room he'd been ushered to made his skin crawl. Racks of frilly little dresses lined the walls on either side of him, and opposite him, piled high on the desk, were literally hundreds of pairs of ruffled panties.

Feeling his muscles tensing in reaction, he forced his gaze away from the intimate apparel and focused on the wall behind the desk. Sketches of curly-headed girls decked out in their Sunday best and little boys dressed up in what Jack could only term Little Lord Fauntleroy outfits—velvet knickers, stockings and patent shoes—covered the wall. He chuckled at the image of his own kids dressed that way. They'd never stand for it. Not for a minute. Ragged sweat suits and dirty sneakers were more their style.

The thought of his kids wiped the smile off his face.

What am I doing here? he asked himself. Teaching young girls party manners in no way guaranteed the woman could teach his kids the same. This had to be the craziest idea he'd ever come up with. Realizing the futility of it, he stood and

,hoved the mug onto the edge of the desk. He was getting
out before he made a complete fool of himself.

In his haste to leave, he knocked a stack of mail from the
desktop to the floor. Cursing his own clumsiness, he knelt
and began to gather it up. He wasn't a nosy man by na-
ure, but he couldn't help noticing that all the envelopes
ooked suspiciously like bills. At closer inspection, the cel-
ophane windows indicated they were all addressed to one
Malinda Compton.

"Jack Brannan is waiting for you in the office."

Frowning slightly, Malinda turned to her business partner. "Jack Brannan? Did he say what he wanted?"

Cecile shrugged as she closed the cash drawer. "Nope.
Just said he needed to talk to you."

Still frowning, Malinda eyed the closed office door, wary.
She could think of only two reasons why a man would visit
her at the store. Knowing this, she sighed deeply as she
moved to join Cecile at the counter. "I certainly hope he's
responding to my ad in the paper and not another repre-
sentative from the collection agency. I'm fresh out of excuses."

"If he's an example of who they're sending out to break
kneecaps these days, I might consider miring myself in
debt."

Malinda couldn't help smiling. "Call a dating service.
Trust me. It's a much more pleasant way to meet men." She
picked up a stack of sales slips from the counter and considered letting the man cool his heels awhile—for all of
about two seconds. Her aunt's voice, as clear as if she stood
in the room with her, admonished her. *Never keep a guest
waiting, Malinda. It's a reflection of ill-breeding.*

"Aunt Hattie, there are days..." Malinda mumbled in
resignation.

Cecile looked up from the cash register receipt she was checking. "Did you say something?"

Malinda shook her head. "Nothing important." She dropped the stack of invoices back onto the counter and drew in a deep breath. "Well, wish me luck. Another thirty-day grace period. That's all I need."

"What you need is to have your head examined for taking on a responsibility that isn't yours."

"Don't start, Cecile," Malinda warned as she headed for the back of the store.

To a stranger, the conversation between the two women might be mistaken for a sign of ill will. Malinda recognized it for what it was—another indication of Cecile's concern. Her business partner's status as childhood friend gave her certain inalienable rights in interfering in Malinda's life, an interference Malinda accepted as readily as she had accepted Cecile's offer of friendship fifteen years before.

Even now Malinda remembered their first meeting as if it had happened yesterday. Two little girls standing on opposite sides of a fence, staring at each other. One dressed in jeans, sneakers and a dirt-smudged T-shirt, the other in a frilly dress, white lacy socks and black patent shoes. Malinda smiled as the memory formed, then faded. As different as night and day. The tomboy and the princess, that's what everyone had called them. Yet despite their differences, the two girls had formed a friendship that had carried them into adulthood and eventually into business together.

At the door to the office she shared with Cecile, Malinda paused, pushing away the memories and focusing her thoughts on the confrontation awaiting her. *They can't draw blood from a turnip,* she reminded herself. *I prom-*

*sed to pay the debts. And I will. They'll just have to be
more patient.*

With her head up, shoulders back, tummy tucked in—
just as Aunt Hattie had daily instructed—she pushed open
the door. For a moment she thought Cecile had been mistaken, for there didn't appear to be anyone in the office.
Then she saw him, crouched down on the floor, his back to
her. And Cecile was wrong. He *was* one of the unsavory
characters the collection agency sent around periodically to
remind her of her debts.

Her first clue was his hair. Like the rest of the agency's
representatives, he obviously had an aversion to barbers.
His hair—almost the same color as his bomber jacket's
aged brown leather—hung well below his collar. Her second clue was his physique. The man was built like a brick
wall. Muscles bunched and strained beneath his jacket with
each of his movements. Her curiosity—and maybe her
temper—piqued, she stepped closer to see just exactly what
the man was doing in *her* office.

"May I help you?"

Guilt. It slammed into Jack with a force of a misguided
beam. In his haste to hide the fact he'd been committing a
federal offense—that of reading another's mail—he lost his
balance and slammed his head against the desk. The mail
clutched in one fist, he rubbed his throbbing forehead with
the flat of his other hand as he slowly spun on the balls of
his feet to face his discoverer.

Directly behind him stood Malinda Compton, Miss Prim
herself. If at a distance she had appeared refined, up close
she was as intimidating as hell. Aristocratic, untouch-
able…totally out of his league. From the tip of her honey-
blond topknot to the soles of her designer shoes, she rep-
resented everything he wasn't. In a word, cultured. He rose

and took an involuntary step backward, thinking only of escape.

She moved closer and extended her hand in greeting. "I'm Malinda Compton. Cecile said you wanted to see me."

The hand extended to him, like the rest of the woman, was graceful and feminine. Reluctantly he took it in his. "Jack Brannan." The softness of her palm made him aware of the calluses on his own while the firmness of her grasp drew his respect. He appreciated both the softness and the strength before she moved behind the desk.

"How may I help you?" she asked as she gestured for him to take the seat opposite her desk.

Reminded of the purpose of his visit, he frowned slightly and dropped back down onto the chair's soft cushions. Help him? Save him would be more accurate. "I'm not sure you can."

His nervous tapping of the letters against the chair's arm caught Malinda's attention. He watched her gaze shift to the miscreant envelopes, and guiltily he leaned forward and dropped them onto her desk. "Sorry. I knocked these off by accident."

Aware of the contents of the envelopes, he could understand the defeated look that flitted across her face before she placed the bills in an open file on her desk. With the closing of the file, her smile returned. "Perhaps if you were to tell me the purpose of your visit, I could make my own assessment."

Again the sweetness of her smile captured him. It didn't just stop at her mouth. It carried all the way to her eyes, making the blue irises sparkle like a lake on a sunny day. And that's where he'd like to be right now, he thought with more than a little resentment. On a lake. Sitting in his boat and fishing for largemouth bass with his sons. But he didn't have the time for fishing. Not until this problem was resolved. And that was why he was here in Malinda Compton's office. *She* was the solution to his problem.

As he continued to meet her gaze, he found something else in her eyes. A friendliness, an invitation for confidences. He fought that temptation. He made it his policy not to trust women. For that matter, he trusted few men. Jack Brannan relied solely on himself. On that philosophy, he had built a construction company from a one-man business to a soon-to-be-reckoned-with company on a national level.

And in order for him to keep that company solvent and growing, he needed to square away his problems on the home front. That reminder made him reconsider his earlier decision to escape this place. Whether he wanted to admit it or not, he needed Malinda Compton. Talking her into teaching his kids, he knew, would be tough. But he had gone up against tougher obstacles and won.

"I'd like to hire you."

With effort, Malinda hid her relief. The man wasn't from the collection agency after all. He had come as a result of her ad. She sent up a silent, but sincere, prayer of thanks for the speedy response to her ad while she pulled a file from her desk drawer. "Here are a list of references and a short résumé for you to review."

Jack waved the offered papers away. "That won't be necessary. Your reputation around town is good enough for me."

The papers dangled limply from Malinda's fingers as she stared at Jack in surprise. "No references?"

Puzzled, Jack asked, "Why would I need references? It's obvious from your column and the success of your classes that you know your stuff."

Malinda dropped the papers back into the folder with a whatever-you-say shrug, but couldn't help adding, "I would think anyone wanting to hire someone to live in their home would check references first."

Jack's puzzlement grew, deepening the frown lines between his eyes. "Live in my home?"

"Well, yes," she said uneasily. "My ad specifically stated I was seeking a live-in housekeeping and baby-sitting position."

Jack chuckled and shook his head. There was a misunderstanding here, and the irony of the situation was almost too much. Three weeks ago he'd been desperate for a live-in housekeeper and baby-sitter and had had a hell of a time finding someone suitable for the job. Not that he considered Mrs. O'Grady, the woman he'd finally hired, totally suitable.

She could cook well enough, keep a path cleared through the house and stay up with the mountains of laundry. But she lacked heart. In his estimation, she didn't give the kids the attention they needed. Not that she didn't see to their welfare. She did that well enough. She just didn't love them. And when it came to teaching the kids any manners, she was as backward as he was, which was why he wanted to hire Malinda. To fill in the gaps, so to speak.

Sensing that Malinda had hopes of more permanent employment than he'd come to offer, Jack offered her an apologetic smile. "Sorry, but I'm not here in response to any ad. I came to see if you'd teach my kids manners."

For a moment, disappointment weighed heavy on Malinda. She quickly dispelled the sensation and focused instead on the positive. Jack Brannan might not want to hire her full-time, but at least he wasn't from the collection agency, and a new student in her etiquette class still meant money in the bank.

She forced a smile and flipped open her desk calendar. "Well, let's see. We've just completed a class today, our next one doesn't begin for six weeks." She picked up a pad of enrollment forms. "If you'll complete an enrollment form and leave a deposit—" In the process of tearing off an application, she glanced up. "You mentioned your children in the plural sense. How many enrollment forms will you need?"

"Four."

She found it difficult to hide the shock his announcement drew. "Four?"

"Yes, four."

Fighting the urge to multiply four times the enrollment fee and mentally add it to her checkbook, she focused on the man in front of her. He certainly didn't look like a father of four. A prizefighter, maybe. The slight crook in his nose suggested it had been broken at least once. Or maybe a construction worker. The width of his shoulders and the muscled breadth of his chest were evidence of some type of physical labor.

Aware she'd been staring, she gave herself a firm mental shake and forced her attention back to the forms. "What are your children's ages?"

"Eight, the twins are five and the youngest is two."

All business now, Malinda thumbed through the forms. "We divide our classes by age group. At the present time we offer a class for preteens, which your oldest would qualify for, and another for young girls, which the twins would qualify for." She smiled an apology. "Unfortunately we don't have a class for toddlers." She tore off three forms and handed them to him.

He handed them right back.

"I don't think you understand. I don't want to enroll my kids in a class." He shook his head and chuckled at a joke only he was privy to. "They wouldn't exactly fit in."

"Some of my students are uneasy at first," she said, anxious to reassure him. "But for the most part, they acclimate quickly."

"Not my kids." Amusement built on his face and finally erupted. He leaned his head back and aimed his laughter at the ceiling. Beneath his darkly tanned skin, his Adam's apple bobbed, drawing Malinda's attention there. She drew in a shocked breath as she realized the circumference of the man's neck probably equaled that of her thigh.

While he continued to laugh at God knew what, Malinda stared. She knew it was rude, Aunt Hattie had taught her that, but she couldn't help herself. She'd never met a man like Jack Brannan before. He had the build of a prizefighter, the self-assurance of a Top Gun pilot and the rugged good looks hyped daily on magazine covers.

While she watched, he slowly sobered, lowering his face to meet her gaze, sending her nerves skittering beneath her skin and making her blush at being caught staring again. He leaned forward and propped his forearms on his thighs, never once moving his gaze from hers. A half smile tugged at one corner of his mouth. "My kids are boys."

The forms slipped from Malinda's fingers and fluttered to the desk. "Boys?" she echoed, her self-consciousness forgotten.

"Yes, boys."

"But I don't teach boys."

"I didn't think you did, but I was hoping you'd consider starting."

Dumbfounded, Malinda sank back against her chair. *Boys?* Pensively she caught her lower lip between her teeth.

"I don't know..." she said, not even trying to disguise her uncertainty.

An etiquette class for boys. The idea had never occurred to her, yet after the initial shock began to wear off, the more she thought about it, the more intriguing she found the proposition.

She'd have to draw up a new format and new lesson plans, but she was sure other parents would be interested in the prospect. Manners—once taught in the home—were quickly becoming a thing of the past. That was why she had developed the class for girls in the first place. But *boys?* She frowned again, considering the possibilities.

Time was a factor. She didn't have any to spare. What with managing the children's store, the classes she already taught and the etiquette column she wrote for the newspaper, she had very little free time. But the prospect of making money was something she couldn't afford to ignore.

If she worked at night, researching the need for manners from a male viewpoint and developing new lesson plans, she could possibly put together a new class within, say, two months. The idea began to take on a certain appeal.

She opened her lap drawer and pulled out paper and pen. "Let me get your telephone number. As soon as I've had a chance to think this through, I'll get back to you."

Jack shook his head. "I don't have time to wait. I need your answer today." When Malinda started to argue the point, he held up a hand to silence her. "I'm willing to pay you well for your time and talents."

She doubted that. His appearance certainly didn't support his statement. Jeans, rugby shirt and a well-worn bomber jacket didn't exactly exude images of unlimited wealth.

Never judge a book by its cover.

Malinda inwardly groaned. Another of Aunt Hattie's little truisms. They haunted her daily. Grudgingly accepting her aunt's reminder, she decided to overlook the man's appearance and focus on another aspect of the problem. "I can't possibly put together a class in one day, and in order to justify my time, I need an enrollment of at least fifteen students, Mr. Brannan."

"Jack," he insisted and scooted his chair closer to the desk.

The movement placed him *too* close for Malinda's comfort. Men were fine at a distance, but when they got too close some innate survival instinct kicked in. Her throat tightened, her hands grew clammy and her eyes refused to blink. Cecile claimed it was Aunt Hattie's fault for constantly preaching that men couldn't be trusted and that a lady must always be conscious of her reputation. Cecile also claimed it was that same philosophy that resulted in Aunt Hattie dying an old maid. Personally Malinda didn't care *whose* fault it was, she just wished she had better control over her body's reactions.

While she discreetly dried her palms on her skirt, Jack smiled at her. For some reason, medicine shows and snake-oil salesmen came to her mind.

"I'm not interested in enrolling my sons in a regular class," he said patiently. "I had more in mind private lessons in my home."

Her fingers stilled on her skirt. "Private lessons? In your home?"

"Yeah. You see, the kids need to have their table manners beefed up a little. I thought you could come over for dinner a couple of nights a week and give them some on-the-spot training, so to speak."

"Mr. Bran—" At his lifted brow, she corrected herself. "—Jack. I appreciate your concern for your children's training, but you must see the impossibility of this proposition."

"Nothing is impossible if you want it badly enough. And believe me, I want this. Besides, this is a no-loss proposition. The boys will learn manners, and you—" he gave the file on her desk a meaningful glance "—will be able to pay off some debts."

Malinda bristled at the reference. "I hardly think the money you could pay me would—"

"How about an even one thousand?"

"—put a dent in—" Her mouth dropped open as his offer registered. "What did you say?"

"A thousand. That's what I'm willing to pay. For the next month and a half you come to my house for dinner three times a week, eat, teach the boys some table manners, stick around afterward for some general pointers, then go home. It's as simple as that."

Malinda's breath returned on an hysterical laugh. "You've got to be kidding."

He sobered her with a piercing look. "I've never been more serious in my life."

"But why?"

He opened his mouth to explain, then clamped it shut again, thinking better of it. "I have my reasons." He leaned back in his chair, templing his fingers together in front of him. "Well? Are you interested?"

A thousand dollars. A couple of hours, three evenings a week for a thousand dollars. She fought the urge to search the room for a hidden camera and Allen Funt. *Candid Camera* had been off the air for years.

Without being conscious of the telling action, Malinda fingered the stack of bills on her desk. A thousand dollars would go a long way toward reducing Aunt Hattie's medical bills. She dropped her hand from the envelopes and mentally shook herself. This was ridiculous. She didn't have time to take on private lessons. And besides, she knew absolutely nothing about this man and even less about teaching little boys etiquette.

But a thousand dollars...

Slowly she raised her gaze to meet his. "I'll do it."

Cecile was still standing at the cash register checking the daily tape when Malinda opened the office door. All too aware of the man who followed her, Malinda led the way through the maze of dress racks and shelving units, purposefully avoiding her partner's curious gaze.

At the store's entrance, Malinda stopped. Jack pulled out a business card, scribbled something on the back and handed it to her.

"My address and my home phone number are on the back. If you have any trouble finding the place, just give me a call."

Already questioning her judgment in accepting his proposition, Malinda stared at the address on the card. "Yes, thank you, I will."

"See you Friday, then."

The bell on the door jingled as Jack swung it open. Cool air hit Malinda's cheeks while the wind caught the hem of her skirt and billowed it out from her legs. Unconsciously she placed a palm against her thigh, holding her skirt in place as she glanced up to watch Jack cross the parking lot.

The same wind that pulled at her skirt caught his hair and blew a lock across his forehead. He raked it back with one hand as he shoved a pair of aviator glasses onto the bridge of his nose with the other. She couldn't help thinking it was a shame to cover up such beautiful eyes.

"What a hunk!"

Yes, Malinda silently concurred as she watched him cross to a Blazer parked next to the street. *What a hunk.* But she didn't dare let on to Cecile that she agreed with her assessment. Cecile would have a field day with that knowledge.

"Was he from the collection agency?"

Malinda watched Jack's thigh muscles bulge, stretching the seams of his jeans as he lifted first one leg, then the other, onto the seat. "No," she replied in a suddenly husky voice.

"Is something wrong?" Cecile asked as she moved to Malinda's side.

Quickly Malinda jerked down the shade over the front door's window, obliterating her view of Jack Brannan. It wouldn't do for Cecile to discover she found the man attractive. She cleared her throat and pasted on a cheerful smile as she turned to face Cecile. "No. Everything's fine."

Cecile frowned as she studied her partner's face. "Yeah, and pigs fly." When Malinda didn't offer anything further, Cecile threw up her hands in exasperation. "Well, if he wasn't from the collection agency, who was he and what did he want?"

Hoping to avoid her friend's penetrating gaze, Malinda moved to a child-size mannequin and fluffed a sleeve that didn't need fluffing. Cecile trailed behind her.

"Well?" she persisted.

"His name is Jack Brannan and he wants me to teach his children etiquette," Malinda replied, still avoiding Cecile's gaze.

"I thought your classes were over for a while?"

"They are. I'll be teaching his children private lessons in their home."

"What!"

Malinda brushed at a piece of lint on the dress's skirt. "I know it's a little unusual, but he offered me a thousand dollars."

Cecile caught Malinda's fidgeting fingers in her own and pulled her friend around to face her. "Now look," she said sternly. "I didn't say anything when you took over Aunt Hattie's manners column in the paper. I could sort of understand the obligation. And I didn't say anything when you started the etiquette classes in the store. You needed the money. And I didn't say *much* when you told me you were going to advertise in the paper for a live-in baby-sitting position so you could lease out Aunt Hattie's house. But this is ridiculous!" She squeezed Malinda's hands hard between her own. "You are going to kill yourself. A person can only do so much."

When Malinda attempted to pull away, Cecile dragged her across the store and positioned her in front of a three-way mirror. "Take a look," she demanded with an impatient wave of her hand. "Take a good look. You're skinny as a rail. Your eyes are bloodshot from lack of sleep, and if it weren't for the concealer you wear, they would have black rings around them that would rival those on a raccoon." She stepped back and folded her arms at her waist. "Now please tell me how you are going to find the strength *or* the time to take on one more project?"

Stricken by her friend's assessment, Malinda stared at her reflection, searching for the telltale signs. Finding them, she sought Cecile's gaze in the mirror. "Is it that obvious?"

Seeing the pain in her friend's eyes, Cecile pulled Malinda into her arms for a quick hug, then pushed her to arm's length. "Only to those who love you." Her expression softened. "Why don't you call your parents and ask them for the money to pay off Aunt Hattie's medical bills? I know they'd give it you."

Malinda dipped her head. "I know that, too." She lifted her head, the message in her eyes begging her friend for understanding. "But I want to do this for Aunt Hattie. She did so much for me."

"That's debatable," Cecile said dryly.

Before Malinda could argue the point, Cecile gave her another quick hug. "I know. I know. In your eyes the woman will always be a saint." She hooked her arm through Malinda's and walked with her to the back of the store. "What about the guy's wife?" she asked. "Why can't she teach the kids some manners?"

"He's a widower."

"Hmm."

Not another word was uttered until they reached the office door—but Malinda could fairly hear the wheels turning in Cecile's head.

"A widower, huh?" Cecile finally said as she pushed open the office door. She folded her arms and pursed her lips thoughtfully as she studied Malinda. "Handsome, single, a body to die for..." She chuckled and gave Malinda a sassy wink. "These private lessons might not be such a bad idea after all."

Two

Jack Brannan's house shocked her. So much so, she was forced to look again at the address he had scrawled on the back of his business card. Yes, she verified, the number on the card matched that displayed in brass on the brick mailbox at the curb. To her shame, she had expected a less prestigious address. Inwardly wincing at her own snobbishness, she shifted her gaze to the house again.

The house might be prestigious, but the lawn surrounding it definitely left a lot to be desired. Thick stands of long-dead weeds seemed to chase the white picket fence that lined the property and huddled against the portion of the house's brick foundation visible from the street. A flurry of wind sent a swirling mass of leaves skittering across the brick drive, drawing Malinda's gaze to the massive pines that dominated the front lawn. Beneath their rich green branches, fallen pine needles lay in deep brown pools. Delight filled her when she discovered redbud trees, smaller and much more delicate than their towering neighbors, scattered among the pines.

Although winter had robbed the lawn of any life, Malinda, always the dreamer, could see beyond the yellow-brown grass and neglect. In her mind's eye, tulips and daffodils surrounded the house, and ivy, thick and trailing, wound its way through the white picket fence.

Forcing her gaze from the lawn, she studied the house. The only word that came to mind was *perfect*. Set back far from the street and partially concealed by the mammoth-sized pine trees, the house built of native stone took on a storybook setting. Enchanted, Malinda turned onto the wide circle driveway, anxious for a closer look.

She stopped her car at the brick sidewalk that curved in a long, lazy S to the front door, then switched off the ignition. Leaning over to peer out the passenger window, she looked again at the house. In the late-afternoon sunlight, the leaded-glass windows that dominated the front reflected the massive pines on a canvas of gold stolen from the sun.

"Okay, Aunt Hattie," she murmured, her gaze still locked on the house. "You were right. I shouldn't have judged the book by its cover." Obviously, if the size and the location of his home were any indication, Jack Brannan was a successful man. Not a man with a green thumb by any stretch of the imagination, but obviously successful if he could afford to live in this neighborhood.

It's not polite to stare, dear. Malinda jerked upright, then laughed. "Aunt Hattie, you're too much."

Quickly gathering her purse, she slipped from the car and headed for the front door, anxious to see if the Brannans were as neglectful with the interior of their home as they were with their lawn.

The front door opened to reveal a sullen-faced boy Malinda assumed to be the eight-year-old Jack had mentioned. In the background, she heard a woman's voice, loud and definitely upset. Offering the child a friendly smile, Malinda extended her hand. "How do you do. I'm Miss Compton."

The child just stood there. After a tense moment of meeting his glare, she withdrew her hand, clutched the shoulder strap of her purse a little bit tighter and tried a different tactic. "Would you tell your father I'm here. He's expecting me."

If possible, the boy's glower drew darker. "He—"

Whatever the child had been about to say was silenced by a flurry of activity and increased shouting. Two more children appeared—undoubtedly the twins, she concluded, since they looked identical—followed by a red-faced, middle-aged woman lugging a suitcase.

"Thank the saints you're here!" The woman dropped the suitcase and jerked a coat from the hall closet. She tugged it on, never once breaking her rhythm. "Babes of the devil himself, they are. A God-fearing woman can take only so much." She tugged a woolen cap over her frazzled hair and, wild-eyed, wheeled to face Malinda. "Raised nine boys of my own, and not one of them," she said, her voice rising hysterically, "ever pulled the tricks these hooligans have played on me."

A car horn sounded out front, and Malinda turned to see a taxi pull up behind her car.

The woman grabbed Malinda's arm and squeezed it hard. Malinda was sure there would be a bruise there the next day.

"The saints be with you, lass. Believe me, you'll need their aid." On that uplifting note, the woman picked up her suitcase, brushed past Malinda and headed for the waiting taxi as if the devil himself were chasing her.

They stood there together, Malinda and the three Brannan boys, and watched the woman throw her suitcase into the back seat of the taxi and climb in after it. After gesturing wildly to the driver, she fell back against the seat and crossed herself with shaking fingers.

Feeling as if she had just stepped into the Twilight Zone, Malinda asked, "Who was that?"

In answer, the eight-year-old slammed the front door and faced Malinda, his arms crossed belligerently over his chest. "Mrs. O'Grady. Our housekeeper."

Though she feared she already knew the answer to her next question, she felt compelled to ask. "Where is your father?"

Before he could reply, the phone rang, and the boy took off down the hall like a shot. Determined to get to the bottom of the situation, Malinda spun to demand the same question of the twins.

They were gone. In the place where they had stood only moments before was the two-year-old, his thumb stuck in his mouth and a blanket hugged tight against his chest. Quickly she scanned the large entry hall, but found no sign of the twins.

A sense of dread filled her. She stooped until she was eye to eye with the two-year-old. "Do you know where your daddy is?" she asked hopefully.

Without a word, he toddled off in the direction his older brother had taken. Not wanting to lose another one, Malinda followed. The toddler stopped in the kitchen beside his oldest brother who was sitting on the kitchen counter, the phone receiver propped between his shoulder and ear while he calmly peeled a banana.

"Mrs. O'Grady just flipped out, Dad. A taxi came and carried her away." The boy was silent for a moment, obviously listening. He glanced up at Malinda and frowned. "Yeah, she's here." He listened a moment longer, then thrust the receiver at Malinda. "Dad wants to talk to you."

"Thank you," she said politely. Careful not to touch the banana smears the child had left on the phone, she accepted the receiver. "Yes?"

"Malinda? It's Jack. Listen. I need a favor. A big one. I'm stuck in Chicago at O'Hare. The airport's closed because of a snowstorm, and now Jack, Jr., tells me Mrs. O'Grady just abandoned ship."

Already suspecting the worst, Malinda asked, "What's the favor?"

"Would you mind staying with the boys until I can get home?"

Thankfully the housekeeper's last warning had not faded from her mind. "Isn't there someone I can call to come and stay with them? A grandmother or an aunt?"

"Not a soul."

Etiquette, she reminded herself. She had been hired to teach etiquette, not baby-sit. And she certainly wouldn't be trapped into playing Mary Poppins to four rowdy boys out of any sense of duty. These children weren't her responsibility. There was a solution to the problem and, given time, she was sure she would think of one.

Her toe tapping out her frustration and her mind whirling, she glanced up and met Jack, Jr.'s, hostile glare. Frowning, she turned her back on him and was confronted with the twoyear-old. His thumb stuck deep in his mouth and his blanket hugged tight to his chest, he stared up at her with the biggest, most pitiful-looking brown eyes she'd ever seen. Immediately her heart turned to peanut butter and her knees to jelly.

The sensation was a familiar one. She experienced it every time she saw a stray dog or cat. Over the years, this fluke in her emotional system had led her to bring home what Aunt Hattie had referred to as a constantly changing menagerie.

Knowing this about herself, how could she possibly walk away and leave these babies unattended?

The banana smears forgotten, she rested her cheek against the receiver, closed her eyes in defeat and murmured, "What time do you think you'll be home?"

"By eight in the morning. That's a promise."

Malinda stood in the bedroom Mrs. O'Grady had recently—and rather hastily, judging by the jumbled looks of things—vacated and stared at the stripes on the bare mattress ticking. She was bone tired and brain dead, not up to searching out clean linens and making up the bed. Her eyes burned, her feet were killing her and she suspected the beginnings of an ulcer were growing in her stomach. And all because of four little boys.

Four little monsters, she clarified in distaste. She fingered the damp towel in her hands and her lips curved into a wistful smile as she remembered the wet hug the two-year-old had given her after she'd bathed him. Well, three monsters. Patrick, the youngest, was definitely a sweetheart.

But his brothers, she reflected with a grimace—*they* were definitely monsters. The past five hours had been a nightmare and not one she was willing to repeat. Dinner had been a fiasco, bath time a free-for-all and bedtime a ritual that would have tried the patience of a saint.

She glanced at the alarm clock on the bedside table and stifled a yawn as she read the illuminated dial. Twelve-thirty. Way past her usual bedtime. And I can't sleep here, she concluded with another look at the bed. Not unless the

Good Fairy appears out of nowhere and makes it up for me. Her shoulders lifted and drooped under the weight of a weary sigh as she turned her back on the uninviting room. The Good Fairy wasn't coming. Malinda knew that. She'd given up on fairy-tale endings long ago.

After checking one last time on the sleeping boys, Malinda found the master bedroom at the end of the hall. Jack hadn't said anything about her sleeping in his room, but under the circumstances, surely he'd understand. Even so, she remained in the doorway, staring at the king-size bed, her lower lip caught between her teeth, unable to take that first bold step inside. She'd never slept in a man's bed before—with or without the man. The thought of doing so now brought a definite uneasiness.

After stealing a guilty glance around, she tiptoed across the room and pressed her fingertips against the mattress. The cushiony spring and the soft, crisp feel of fresh linens were too much to resist. And he won't be home until morning, she reminded herself. An early riser, she knew she'd be up, dressed and out of his room prior to his return. Before she could change her mind, she flung back the bedspread, pulled back the sheet and fluffed the pillow.

Ignoring Jack's offer over the phone of one of his T-shirts as sleepwear, she quickly stripped, then pulled back on her full slip as a nightgown. As was her habit, she neatly folded her clothes and stacked them on a chair before crossing to the bed.

A woman should never place herself in a situation that would compromise her reputation.

Malinda froze with one foot still planted on the floor but the opposite knee and both hands buried in Jack Brannan's bed. Her head sagged between her elbows. "Oh, Aunt Hattie, please," she murmured wearily. Reluctantly she pushed to her feet and stared longingly at the bed. She was so-o-o tired and the bed looked so-o-o comfortable.

"So what's wrong with me sleeping in his bed?" she asked the empty room. "Nothing. Absolutely nothing," she answered. Squaring her shoulders in a rare act of defiance, she glanced up at the ceiling. "Rest easy, Aunt Hattie," she said and climbed between the sheets. "I intend to."

Turning her cheek against the soft down of the pillow, she breathed a sigh of sheer pleasure. Rest. That's what she needed. In the morning the world would appear brighter. Jack would return, she would renege on her agreement to teach his children manners and she could resume her life once again—minus her obligation to the four Brannan boys, of course.

Snowflakes as big as quarters splattered against the windshield of Jack Brannan's Blazer as he pulled from the covered parking garage at Will Rogers Airport. He frowned at them and switched on the wipers. He'd had about all the snow he could stomach in Chicago and now it appeared he was going to have to put up with more of the same in Oklahoma City.

But he should be thankful, he told himself. If not for a break in the storm and O'Hare's efficient snow crews, he'd still be sitting in the Chicago airport, drinking lukewarm coffee and twiddling his thumbs, not on his way home. But as hard as he tried, Jack couldn't work up any gratitude. He was too damn tired.

The drive from the airport to his home in Edmond took less than twenty minutes. It should have taken at least thirty, but Jack was in a hurry. Fortunately traffic on the expressway was light due to the late hour and the snow hadn't built up enough to impede his speed.

And Malinda Compton was home with his boys. That thought alone had him pressing down harder on the accelerator. He didn't like to ask people for favors. Being indebted to another individual didn't sit well with him at all. Jack Brannan handled his own problems and had for years.

He'd pay her for her services, he decided with a satisfied nod at the windshield, then he wouldn't be in her debt. She needed the money and he needed someone to stay with his kids until he could get home. An even trade, to his way of thinking.

When he turned onto his driveway, the porch light cut an inviting swath across the front lawn and, as he circled around to the garage, he saw that the light above the kitchen sink burned, as well. A warm feeling spread across his chest, melting away his impatience as well as the cold. Home. He was finally home.

Warm air greeted him when he pushed open the back door and stepped into the kitchen. Home, he thought again, absorbing that simple pleasure as he glanced around the dimly lit room.

His fingers tensed on the knob.

He blinked hard and looked again. His first thought was that he was in the wrong house. Instead of the disaster area he usually found on his arrival home, the room was neat as a pin. The table was wiped clean, no dirty dishes were stacked in the sink and the floor shined like the top of Jim McIntire's—his site supervisor's—bald head. He glanced down at his feet to the slush he had tracked in and immediately stepped back onto the porch and scraped his snow-caked boots against the mat on the stoop.

After closing and locking the door behind him, he strode across the kitchen, switched off the light above the sink and headed down the back hall. Somewhere in this house he knew he'd find his kids, hog-tied and gagged. There could be no other explanation.

Even in the darkness he could see that the rest of the house matched the order he'd found in the kitchen. No toys strewn about the den for him to trip over. No bikes, trucks or trikes blocking his path in the hallway.

At the hall bath, he paused and looked in. No wet towels hung from the shower rod, no clothes littered the floor. For a second, he forgot his intention to find his sons and admired the tile work on the bathroom floor. His work. His creation. But when was the last time he'd even seen the bathroom floor?

This isn't normal, he thought, dragging a shaky hand through his already mussed hair. Something's not right. His imagination working overtime, he headed for the back of the house and Mrs. O'Grady's room, hoping to find Malinda and put his mind at ease. What he found there stopped him cold. The bed was not only empty, it was bare as a newborn baby's behind.

His heart pounding in his chest, he swung around and headed for the east wing of the house and his sons' rooms. In the time it took to cross from one end of the house to the other, he convinced himself that Malinda Compton was a crazed kidnapper who used her children's shop as a front for a black-market adoption agency.

At Jack, Jr.'s, room he stopped and peered in. Spread-eagled on the bed with the comforter twisted around his upper body, his oldest son slept with one arm draped across his eyes. One bare foot hung off the side of the bed. Jack sagged against the door frame in relief. Thank God they're safe, he thought, laughing at his own foolishness.

After his heart had slowed its fearful pounding, he pushed away from the frame and crossed the room to tuck his son's foot back under the comforter. Looking down at the boy, he felt his chest swell with pride. Like father, like son, he thought as he straightened the comforter around his son's slim body. He, too, was hot natured and usually kicked off his covers no matter how cold the night.

One down, three to go. He crossed the hall to the twins' room. The bunk beds, although mussed, were empty. All his fears resurged. Wheeling around, he charged for the baby's room. The soft glow of Patrick's night-light revealed that his youngest son's bed, too, was empty.

Why would she take the three little ones and leave the oldest? he asked himself. Because younger ones are easier to adopt out, you fool. Your own experience should have taught you that.

Desperate now, he started to wake Jack, Jr., and demand some answers but thought better of it. No sense in upsetting the boy until he had facts to support his theory. The police. He'd call the police. They'd know what to do. The nearest phone was in the master bedroom and he took off at a fast run.

Not bothering with a light, he grabbed the telephone from the nightstand, and at the same time, dropped down onto the bed. A surprised "Umph!" had him jumping back to his feet and twisting around to peer behind him. A sleepy-eyed Darren smiled up at him from the bed. "Hi, Dad," the boy mumbled.

Hiding his fear behind a wall of impatience, Jack slammed the phone back on the nightstand. "What are you doing in here?" he whispered through tight lips.

"Me and David had a bad dream, so we came in here to sleep."

His hand still shaking, Jack groped for the lamp and switched it on. Besides Darren and David, two more lumps were visible in the soft lamplight, one tiny one and one decidedly curvaceous one.

Darren yawned. "Is it time to get up?"

"No, not yet." For a moment Jack considered leaving the boys where they were and climbing in beside them. But only for a moment. He knew what it was like to sleep with his sons. They kicked like mules. "Come on," he said wearily and pulled back the covers. "I'll carry you boys to your beds."

He scooped up Darren and tossed him over his shoulder in a fireman's carry, then snuggled the still-sleeping David against his chest. After depositing the twins in their bunks, he headed back to his room, stripping his sweater over his head as he went.

He crawled across the bed, eased Patrick into his arms without waking him and carried him back to his room.

When he returned, he stood for a moment, hands on hips, and studied Malinda's sleeping form. Asleep, she looked as innocent and as youthful as his kids. Nothing at all like the prim and proper woman he'd met the day he'd hired her.

Her hair, which he remembered from their first meeting as being twisted up in a bun, now draped across one cheek and cascaded over her shoulder and down her back. One bare shoulder rose and fell in the relaxed rhythm of sleep.

Hypnotized by her shoulder's movement, Jack stood, unmoving. Fully dressed, Malinda Compton was a lady through and through. Half-naked and lying in his bed, she was a temptress. He shifted his gaze to her mouth. Moist and full, her lips, relaxed in sleep, formed a soft pout.

His own mouth went dry. More than anything in the world he wanted to crawl in beside her and cuddle up.

She moaned, startling him, and rolled to her back. The movement tugged the blanket to her waist, exposing a generous view of cleavage and lace. Jack's breath lodged somewhere in his chest. *A lady,* he reminded himself firmly and tightened his hands into fists at his sides. *And one who wouldn't appreciate your getting an eyeful while she slept.*

Focusing on the problem at hand, he tried to decide what to do. He hated to wake her. Obviously she was beat, considering she'd slept through the transfer of the kids to their own rooms. He considered just picking her up as he had the boys, but if he did, where would he put her? Mrs. O'Grady's bed wasn't made and he knew from experience the couch in the den was about as comfortable as sleeping on a slab of steel.

And after a week of hotel rooms *he* sure as hell wasn't sleeping anywhere but in his own bed. He glanced across the wide expanse of unused bed, then back to Malinda. Shrugging his shoulders, he crossed to the opposite side, stripped off his boots, socks and jeans, then crawled under the covers.

Hell, she'd never even know he was there.

Malinda felt as if her back was on fire. More asleep than awake, she inched away from the inferno behind her and snuggled her cheek deeper into the pillow. Immediately the heat returned. And a cinch at her waist, as well. One by one, as she struggled to wakefulness, she determined other strange sensations. A moist warmth at her neck, a pressure at her back and again behind her knees.

None of the sensations was altogether unpleasant. In fact, there was an odd sense of security in it all. Was it a dream? In an attempt to focus her thoughts, she opened her eyes and studied the wall opposite her. This isn't my room, she thought in confusion. Lifting her head slightly, she glanced around until her gaze rested on the chair in the corner and her carefully folded clothes.

Closing her eyes in resignation, she remembered where she was and what she was doing there. Jack Brannan's house. Baby-sitting his four little monsters. And one of the little monsters was fixing to lose an arm if he didn't scoot over and give her some room in the bed, she thought irritably.

Brushing her hair back from her face, she turned to confront the guilty monster... and met the heavy-lidded gaze of Jack Brannan. "What are you doing here?" she gasped in a hoarse whisper.

He smiled a slow, sleepy smile. "I could ask you the same question."

Scooting away from him, she clutched the sheet to her breasts. "Get out."

One thick eyebrow arched into a neat V. "Get out?" he repeated.

"Yes! Get out."

Robbed of his cover, he tucked his hands beneath his armpits, closed his eyes and settled his head more comfortably against the pillow. "It's my bed. If anybody's getting out, it's you."

Angered by his refusal, Malinda flung back the covers, then remembering she wore only a slip, grabbed them and pulled them to her chin. Flat on her back, pinned to the bed by her embarrassment, she stared up at the ceiling, her face throbbing to beat the band. "I can't. I'm not dressed."

"Neither am I."

Without thinking, Malinda twisted her head to look at him and was greeted by a bare, hair-shadowed chest. When her gaze reached his waist and a stretch of white elastic, she squeezed her eyes shut and swallowed hard as she turned her face back to the ceiling. "So now what do we do?" she whispered in a shaky voice.

"I don't know about you, but I'm going back to sleep."

She felt the quiver of his muscles through the mattress as he stretched, then the weight of his arm as he circled her

waist again, and lastly his breath as he moved his head to
share her pillow.

In a heartbeat she was up, standing beside the bed, her
breasts heaving, the comforter she'd dragged from the bed
wrapped tight around her body. "You—you animal!" she
screeched. She stomped across the room to the chair and
gathered her clothes to her breasts.

At the door, she jerked to a halt and wheeled to face him.
Even in the darkness, he could see the anger sparking in her
eyes. "My responsibilities to your children are at an end. If
they need a glass of water, or have to use the rest room, or
have a nightmare, or any of the other thousand excuses they
find to get out of bed, *you'll* see to their needs. I'm
through!"

"Malinda?"

Already in midturn, she whipped back around. "What!"
she demanded.

"Where are you going?"

"Home! I wouldn't stay another minute in this madhouse if my life depended on it."

"Do you have a four-wheel drive?"

The absurdity of the question loosened her grip on the
comforter. She snatched it tighter beneath her arm and
lifted her chin another notch before demanding, "And
what does *that* have to do with anything?"

He opened one eye and smiled at her. "Without four-
wheel drive you won't make it to the end of the driveway.
It's been snowing for hours." He patted the space beside
him. "Why don't you come back to bed and I'll take you
home in the morning?"

"Back to bed!" She sucked in an indignant breath, then
marched back across the room. Wrenching the pillow from

beneath his head, she said in a voice laced with enough venom to kill, "A lady does not share a bed with a man without the privilege of marriage. And I'll have you know I'd sleep in the bathtub before I'd share a bed with you!"

Three

———

"No, you can't wake her up." Jack caught the toast as it popped from the toaster, then slathered it with jelly before dropping it onto a plate.

"But it's almost nine. She'll miss all the cartoons."

Jack chuckled and shoved the plate into Darren's hand. "Something tells me Miss Compton will survive a morning without cartoons."

After pouring himself a mug of coffee, he joined the boys at the table. "How'd it go last night?"

Jack, Jr., backhanded the chocolate-milk mustache from his upper lip with his sweatshirt sleeve. "Okay, I guess."

Jack smiled encouragingly. "Well, did you learn anything?"

His oldest son eyed him warily. "Like what?"

"Like manners, for cripes sake! The lady came to teach you boys some manners." He glanced around the table and caught the warning look his oldest son shot the twins.

"Okay, boys," he said on a sigh. "Let's have it. What did y'all do to Miss Compton?"

"Short of tying me to a funeral pyre and striking a match, you mean?"

Jack whirled to find Malinda standing in the kitchen doorway, her gaze leveled on the boys. Miss Prim was back. She'd pulled up her hair into the neat bun he remembered from their first meeting and she was fully dressed. A very different picture from the woman who had greeted him in the wee hours of the morning.

That woman's hair had been down, wild tangles that had cascaded halfway down her back. He could still remember how she'd looked when he'd suggested she get back in bed. Her chin had lifted in indignation, her breasts had swelled, pushing at the thin silk that covered them. With an angry swipe of a manicured hand, she had tossed the tangled mass of honey-blond hair over her shoulder and leveled him with a look that told him just where she thought he could place his suggestion.

Biting back a smile, he decided he liked the slightly mussed Miss Prim better than this piece of perfection.

"Not much," she finished as she strode purposefully into the room, her back straight, her shoulders square and her chin held high enough to catch water.

At the coffeepot she stopped. "You might have warned me, you know," she suggested as she poured herself a cup. Without turning, she touched the cup to her lips and blew softly. "If I'd known I'd be dealing with juvenile delinquents, I wouldn't have been so hasty in agreeing to stay with them."

Jack stole a glance at his sons' downcast faces, then frowned at Malinda's back. "What did they do?"

"Do?" she echoed in a musical voice edged with sarcasm. She whirled to face the culprits. She knew her Aunt

Hattie would die if she were present to hear Malinda's lack of manners, but at the moment Malinda didn't care. These boys had put her through hell and it was time to even the score. Crossing the room, she tapped one of the twins on the shoulder. "Why don't you ask Darren here?"

Accustomed to the mix-up with the twins, Jack waved a hand in their direction and corrected her. "That's not Darren. That's David."

Malinda looked from Darren to David and back again, sure she wasn't mistaken. The night before, after they had driven her up the wall for hours by confusing her with their names, she had put David in red pajamas and Darren in blue so she could tell them apart. Suspecting they'd had the last word after all, she lowered her face to meet Darren's eye. "What's your name?"

"David," he mumbled and attempted to avoid her gaze.

"And is that the same name you gave me last night when I helped you into your pajamas?"

He stole a glance at his father's disapproving frown and slid farther down in his chair. "No."

Malinda folded her arms at her waist and smiled a self-righteous smile. "I rest my case."

"They were just having a little fun, that's—"

"A little fun?" Malinda whirled to face Jack, all the indignities she'd suffered the night before coming to a head. "I'll tell you what fun is. Unclogging a toilet jammed with three rolls of tissue paper. Cleaning Vaseline petroleum jelly off every doorknob in the house. Listening to three boys burp their way through dinner like some beer-besotted imbeciles."

She drew in a ragged breath to continue, but quickly swallowed her list of grievances when Jack scraped back his chair and rose. His height was intimidating enough, but

combined with the breadth of his shoulders and the angry
slice of his lips, Malinda was properly subdued.

With a leveling look that encompassed all four children,
he said in a voice that brooked no argument, "Boys, go to
your rooms and wait for me there."

One by one, the three oldest pushed away from the table. With their heads hanging low, the twins slunk from the
room while Jack, Jr., freed Patrick from his high chair. At
the kitchen door, Jack, Jr., stopped and glanced back at
Malinda. The look he shot her would have melted paint off
a wall. Remembering his obstinateness and rudeness the
night before, she stiffened her spine and shifted her gaze to
the little one he carried in his arms.

The look Patrick gave her melted her heart. She closed
her eyes against the pitiful sight of the retreating brothers,
huddled together in their misery. They were in big trouble
and they knew it. And worse... she knew it.

"I'm sorry for the way the boys acted," Jack said, his
voice tight. "I'd like to lie and say they aren't always this
bad, but—well, hell, they usually are. But I promise you
they'll be punished for what they put you through."

Jack's final announcement jolted her attention away
from the boys and back to their father. Standing less than
an arm's length away, he appeared so much bigger than
those little boys. A mental picture of him punishing them
blinded her to the little demons' faults.

Emotion clogged her throat and she found she was unable to respond. It was her fault the boys were in trouble.
Her fault they were probably about to get the spanking of
their lives. If only she hadn't been so quick to tattle on their
bad behavior.

It's never too late to right a wrong. Aunt Hattie again.
Malinda didn't even attempt to thwart the unrequested advice. She'd been raised on Aunt Hattie's truisms to the

point that, even after her guardian's death, Aunt Hattie's strict teachings still came to mind. As much as she'd hated hearing them while growing up, as an adult she had learned to appreciate their wisdom.

Mindful of that fact, she pasted on an understanding smile. "The boys weren't really *that* bad. I'm just tired. It was an awfully long night. And I'm not accustomed to little boys." She knew she was babbling, grasping at straws to keep him from disciplining the children, but she couldn't stop herself. "And as you said, they were just having a little fun."

Jack's frown deepened as he stacked the breakfast dishes. "Fun's one thing. Harassment's another. I won't have the boys showing disrespect to an adult." After placing the dishes beside the sink, he turned to Malinda. The sternness of his expression was enough to make her quake in her boots. "If you don't mind waiting, as soon as I take care of the boys I'll drive you home."

When he disappeared from sight, Malinda collapsed onto a chair and pressed her hands over her ears. Those poor little boys. She couldn't bear to hear them cry. And it was all her fault.

She sat that way—elbows on knees, palms pressed flat against her ears, eyes squeezed shut—for what seemed like an eternity. And heard nothing. Gradually she eased her hands from her ears. Still, she heard nothing. No loud voices, no crying.

This is ridiculous! she lectured herself and pushed to her feet. She had to do something, anything, so she didn't focus on what was transpiring at the other end of the house. Rolling up her sleeves, she headed for the pile of dirty dishes. With her hands buried in soapy water, she realized that although her hands were busy her ears weren't. She was still listening for sounds from the other end of the house. So she started humming.

And that's how Jack Brannan and his sons found her. Standing at the kitchen sink with soap bubbles to her elbows, scrubbing plates hard enough to take the ceramic finish off and humming loud enough to wake the dead. Jack had to call her name three times before she finally heard him over the racket she was creating.

Startled, she wheeled to find him standing behind her. Patrick was perched on his hip. "My gracious!" she said, pressing soapy hands to her breasts. "You scared the life out of me."

"Sorry, but you were making so much racket you didn't hear me the first couple of times I called." Jack shifted Patrick to the opposite hip and motioned for the other three to join him. "The boys have something to say to you."

Obediently they shuffled forward, their heads hanging low. Malinda swallowed hard and blinked even harder to hold back her tears. She'd rather drink a bottle of castor oil—Aunt Hattie's cure for most ailments—than go through with this.

"We're sorry, Malinda," they mumbled in unison.

Seeing they were as uncomfortable in this situation as she was, she smiled encouragingly. "I'm sure you didn't mean any harm. Apology accepted."

Jack placed a hand on Jack, Jr.'s, shoulder. "Since Malinda was the one offended by your pranks, it's only fair that she decide the punishment."

Malinda snapped her head up to meet his gaze. "What?" she gasped.

"Their punishment. It's up to you."

"But they apologized. Isn't that enough?"

"Not in my book. They caused you a lot of unnecessary work, therefore they have to pay the price."

She knew he was right. But heavens! She knew absolutely nothing about delving out punishments. As she stood there, unsure what to do or say, the weight of the boys' expectant gazes began to weigh on her.

Stalling for time, she took a dish towel from the counter and slowly dried her hands as she struggled to come up with an idea—anything!—so they'd all quit staring at her.

The punishment should equal the crime. Malinda sent up silent thanks to Aunt Hattie.

"Okay," she said, her voice filled with more self-confidence than she felt. "Darren, you and David are the two who stopped up the commode with tissue paper, so perhaps a good lesson for you would be for you to clean the bathroom floor. With a toothbrush," she added as an afterthought.

She shifted her attention to Jack, Jr. He might have offered an apology, but the surly expression on his face suggested that it had not come from the heart. His punishment would be harder to determine, for what punishment would equal his crime, that of disrespect and lack of compassion in a situation where he knew she was definitely out of her element?

She glanced out the window, her gaze traveling from the snowdrifts stacked against the garage and along the driveway to the neighboring house beyond. Suddenly a thought occurred to her. "Who lives in the house next door?" she asked Jack, Jr.

"The Morgans."

"Do they have children?"

"Yeah, five."

Well, there went that idea. Frustrated, she pressed her lips together. "Okay, so who lives across the street?" she demanded impatiently.

Jack, Jr., rolled his eyes. "Old Lady Harris."

Malinda lifted one eyebrow. Bingo! "Old Lady Harris?" she repeated. "Does she live alone?"

Jack, Jr., blew out a disbelieving breath. "Who'd live with her? She's crazy as a bat."

"Well, thank goodness you don't have to live with her. You just have to shovel the snow off her sidewalk."

"What! Her sidewalk's a mile long."

Pursing his lips to hide his amusement, Jack gave his son a gentle push. "Not quite a mile. Your snowsuit and gloves are in the laundry room closet. And you'll find the snow shovel hanging on the wall rack in the garage." He turned to the twins. "You guys each get an old toothbrush out of the bottom drawer in your bathroom and get busy."

When the boys were gone, Jack jiggled Patrick on his hip. "Down to this one. What's his punishment?"

Relieved the worst was over, Malinda laughed. "Forty lashes with a wet noodle." She stretched out her hands and Patrick fell into them. When he wrapped his arms around her neck and buried his nose just beneath her ear, she closed her eyes and hugged him back, savoring the smell of the baby powder she herself had dusted him with the night before.

She opened her eyes to find Jack frowning at his son's back. The look was oddly disconcerting and immediately she loosened her hold on Patrick. "I hope you don't think my punishments for the boys too severe. I'm not used to doing this sort of thing."

"No. You did just fine." Jack reached for Patrick without looking at her. "I'll go put him down for his nap."

Puzzled by Jack's odd behavior, Malinda busied herself in the kitchen. When he returned, she was at the sink, rinsing the breakfast dishes.

He took the plate she was scrubbing from her hand. "I didn't expect you to clean up after us."

"Oh, I don't mind." She glanced wistfully around, thinking of the outdated and cramped kitchen at Aunt Hattie's house—her house now. "To be honest, it's a joy to work in such a large and modern kitchen. The newest appliance in mine is a twelve-year-old electric can opener."

"All the same, it's not expected." Jack leaned behind her, planting a hand at her waist for balance as he stretched to place the plate in the dishwasher rack.

Malinda's eyes widened and her stomach muscles tightened at the contact. Sensations, mirroring those she'd awakened to earlier that morning, spiraled through her. His hand at her waist, his body pressed flat against her back. No man had ever touched her so casually, yet so intimately. No man had ever dared come this close.

Her hands found the edge of the sink and clung.

"You did a good job dishing out the boys' punishments." He was standing beside her again. Slowly Malinda relaxed her grip on the sink. He chuckled, then added, "I think they'll think twice before they try any pranks on you again."

She snapped her head around to stare at him. *Again?* Surely he didn't expect her to teach his children after the fiasco the night before? If ever anyone was beyond hope, it was the Brannan boys. How could she gracefully remove herself from this obligation? Slipping her hands beneath the soapy dishwater, she pulled out another plate. "About our arrangement," she began. Nervously she cleared her throat, unsure how to broach the subject without hurting his parental pride.

Jack took the plate from her hand and nudged her to the side with his hip. "I hope the boys' pranks haven't scared you off?"

Malinda watched helplessly as he scrubbed at the jelly-smeared plate. "Scared me off?" she repeated. She waved a negligent hand and laughed, but even to her own ears the laugh lacked conviction. "Heavens, no! It's just that—well, it's just that I don't think I have the time or the skills to truly help them," she explained. "You see, boys are *so* different from girls."

Jack sucked in one cheek and gave her a slow, appraising look. "Oh, really? I hadn't noticed."

His bold, familiar look reminded her she'd spent at least part of the night in the man's bed, half-dressed, and with his arm locked around her waist. She felt the blood rush to her face. She snatched the plate from his hand and angled it onto the dishwasher rack. "Couldn't your mother work with the boys?" she asked impatiently.

"And which mother would you suggest I ask?"

Malinda straightened with a start. "You have more than one?"

"Seven. No make that eight," he corrected as he passed her a glass.

Suspecting he was teasing her, Malinda held the glass up to the window and frowned. "Sure you do." Finding a milk ring on the glass she handed it back.

"I do have eight mothers." He stuffed the dishcloth into the glass and gave it several brisk twists. "Mrs. Carothers, Mrs. Givens, Mrs. Lightfoot, Mrs. Kern, Mrs. Brown, Mrs. Bowman, Mrs. Smith and Mrs. Pringle." He handed the glass back.

"There seems to be one name missing," she said dryly. "Mrs. Brannan."

"True, but she doesn't qualify as a mother."

Frustrated with the riddle-filled conversation, Malinda shoved the glass onto the rack, then folded her arms at her breasts. "And how does a mother *not* qualify as a mother?"

"When she gives her child away to the state."

The cold, emotionless statement chilled Malinda to the bone. She knew how it felt to have absentee parents, but didn't have a clue as to how it felt to be given away. Regretting her earlier sarcasm, she asked softly, "How old were you?"

"Ten. Too old to attract couples who wanted to adopt and too young to go out on my own." His hands dripping with dishwater, he lifted a wrist to his cheek and rubbed at his jaw.

Malinda watched his wrist's journey from the gentle curve of his ear down the sharp line of his jaw to his chin and back again. The gesture was all adult male, but Malinda couldn't help thinking of the innocent ten-year-old boy abandoned by his parents. When his gaze met hers, she detected a shadow of the pain he must have experienced. "I'm sorry," she offered softly. "That must have been awful for you."

Jack had seen it coming. First in her eyes, then in the slight quiver of her lips. Pity. God, how he hated it.

Tearing his gaze from hers, he dunked his hands back into the dishwater. "I survived," he replied curtly as he pulled out the plug.

While he waited for the water to drain, he glanced out the window. Across the street, he could see Jack, Jr., shoveling away at Old Lady Harris's snow-clogged sidewalk. His heart swelled until he thought it would burst and his throat tightened, nearly choking him.

Damn those teachers to hell and back, he thought angrily. His boys were good kids. A little rough around the edges, maybe, but good kids. It wasn't their fault they didn't have a mother to teach them social graces any more than it was his fault he didn't know enough to teach.

But they had a father, he thought with determination, and their father could damn well afford to provide them with everything he'd missed out on as a kid. He needed help, that was all. And help you could buy.

He stole a glance at Malinda, who stood at his side, her gaze fixed on the snowy scene outside. Her head was up, her back straight as a board, her hands folded neatly on the countertop. Miss Prim. The perfect person for the job.

Earlier, when he'd seen how easily Patrick had fallen into her arms, an idea had occurred to him—a crazy one, but an idea all the same. Malinda was younger than he'd like for the job, fragile looking and way too persnickety, but Patrick liked her and she obviously liked him. And judging by the looks of the house after only one night there, she could handle the housekeeping duties. Two birds with one stone. Someone to teach the kids manners and a new housekeeper and baby-sitter, all rolled into one.

He touched his hand to the small of her back and guided her to the kitchen table and pulled out a chair. He'd learned long ago it was usually best to act on gut instincts. Taking the seat opposite her, he said, "When I was in your office the other day you mentioned something about an ad in the paper."

Her thoughts still centered on the deprivation in Jack Brannan's youth, she replied absently, "Yes, I'm seeking employment as a live-in housekeeper and baby-sitter."

"Why?"

Sighing, she smoothed the wrinkles from her skirt's front, then clasped her hands on the tabletop. Immediately she tensed, regretting the move. Her hands now rested only inches from Jack's. Fisted, his looked huge. And strong. Sun-bleached hair dusted the backs of his hands and shadowed his arms to the edges of the sleeves he'd cuffed just below his elbows. The old survival instinct kicked in. Her throat dried up, her palms began to perspire and her eyes burned from her inability to blink.

"Malinda?"

She jerked her gaze from where it rested on his hands. Not wanting him to know how his proximity affected her, she cleared her throat and slipped her hands to her lap. "Excuse me?" she said, fighting for time to gather her wits.

"I said, 'Why?' Why do you want another job? It looks to me like you've got your hands full with your store, your classes and that column you write for the paper."

"True. I do have plenty to keep me busy. I just don't have plenty of money."

"Well, if you're so busy, how would you find time to baby-sit and keep a house?"

"In my ad I specifically requested school-age children. Since the store doesn't open until ten, I'd have time to get the children ready for school, straighten the house and still arrive at the store in time to open up for the day." She laughed softly, thinking of her partner and their arrangement. "Cecile is not a morning person, so by mutual agreement I take the morning responsibilities and she the afternoon. That means I would be free by the time the children got out of school to take them to any extracurricular activities."

The fact that she only wanted school-age children presented a problem, but Jack wasn't ready to let go of this gut feeling yet. He laced and unlaced his fingers a moment, studying them intently before he lifted his gaze to Malinda's. "What if someone approached you who had a child who wasn't of school-age? Would you be able to work out some kind of an arrangement?"

His expression was so intense Malinda found it almost unnerving. "I don't know," she replied slowly, unable to look away. "I suppose if the parents were in agreement, the child could go to work with me. Sometimes Cecile brings her children to the shop. We have a play area set up with toys and tables for coloring.''

The tension in Jack's face melted away. ''Great!'' he yelled and slapped the table hard with the palm of his hand. ''So how would you like to go to work for us?''

Malinda grabbed the edge of the table for support. *Work for the Brannans? Full-time?* She'd already decided she couldn't bear to be in their presence the couple of hours a week required to teach them etiquette, and he wanted her to *live* with them? The very suggestion was so preposterous she was left speechless.

The look on Malinda's face was enough to let Jack know the idea didn't sound so ''great'' to her. But damn it, he needed her and his boys needed her. And judging by the stiffness of her spine and the purse of her lips, she needed them, too, to teach her how to let her hair down a little, to take a little of the starch out of her panties, so to speak.

Given the time, he knew he could persuade her to stay with them, to make her see it would be a mutually profitable arrangement. Quickly, before she had a chance to refuse his offer, he reached out and grabbed her hand. ''You don't have to give me an answer now,'' he assured her. He squeezed her hand, then released it to gesture toward the window. Snow was falling again. ''Since the weather's so bad, why don't you spend the rest of the day with us? Kind of get to know us better. Then you can decide. I'll take you home in the morning, first thing, I promise.''

Brown eyes, so penetrating they were almost mesmerizing, held Malinda's blue ones. This man was dangerous. She could feel it in her bones. How could she possibly live in the same house with him when she couldn't even breathe with him this close? She swallowed hard and tore her gaze from his to glance out the window. She rubbed her hands together in her lap. The one still burned from his touch.

She knew she was insane to even consider the idea. The Brannan boys were more than she could handle. And their father...he was *definitely* more than she could handle. But all she could think about was the precious feel of Patrick's little arms wrapped around her neck, this beautiful house that needed a woman's touch...and the warmth of Jack Brannan's hand on hers.

Shaking her head to clear the tempting thoughts, she turned back to Jack. "I couldn't really. I don't have any clothes—"

"It's just for one day."

"And I really need to work on my column for the newspaper. It's due—"

"You can use my study here at the house. I promise we won't bother you."

"My house—"

"Will still be there tomorrow." One side of his mouth quirked up in a grin. A grin Malinda was discovering very hard to refuse. "What's one day? Say you'll stay."

Four

With one fatal swoop of a hand, Jack scraped the litter that cluttered his desk into his arms and dumped it all into a disorganized heap on the floor.

"Just make yourself at home," he said as he pulled out the desk chair for Malinda. "Typing paper is in the top right drawer. Pencils and pens are here," he said, tapping the drawer just above her knees. "If you need anything else, just holler."

He took one last look around, offered Malinda one of his hard-to-resist grins and closed the door behind him.

She glared at the closed door. The rat! How had he talked her into this? Two hours ago she'd had no intention of staying another minute in this house, much less the night, and yet here she sat behind *his* desk!

She propped her elbows on the desk and her chin in her hands. She had too much to do to get involved with the Brannans. She didn't have the experience necessary to deal with four young boys. And she certainly didn't have the experience to handle a charmer like Jack Brannan.

He'd promised her an hour of uninterrupted silence so she could work on her column. She knew she needed that and more. Emitting a deep sigh, she lifted her elbows from the desk. Or at least she tried to. Something gummy and sticky clung to her sleeves. Grimacing, she tugged herself free.

It took fifteen minutes to clean the rubber cement from the desk. Another ten to straighten the drawer where the typewriter paper was stored. A search through the lap drawer for a pen that would write convinced her Jack Brannan was anything but neat. Without thinking twice about whether he would approve or not, she methodically began to clean and organize.

When Jack stepped into the office an hour later, he found Malinda, her sleeves rolled to her elbows, straggles of hair hanging limp from her bun, a smudge of ink staining one cheek.

And his office, spotless.

"What the hell are you doing?"

Bent over a much-ignored fig tree, pruning away dead leaves, Malinda jerked upright. When she saw him in the doorway, his hands fisted and resting on his hips, she closed her eyes and placed a hand over her heart. "I do wish you would warn a person before you enter a room."

He strode into the study, glancing this way and that. "What have you done with all my stuff?"

The accusatory tone in his voice didn't daunt Malinda. Organizing and cleaning always put her on a high. "Put it away. Everything has a place and every place a thing," she recited cheerfully, quoting her Aunt Hattie.

"I thought you were going to work on your column?"

"I was. But first I had to prize my arm off your desk. Rubber cement, I believe," she said pointedly. "As soon as I removed that mess, I intended to begin, but then I couldn't find the typing paper for all the clutter in the drawer." She pulled out the drawer in question. Everything inside was sorted, stacked and aligned military straight.

The woman was unbelievable. *But I need her,* he reminded himself. Fighting for calm, knowing full well he'd never be able to find a damn thing in his study again, he forced a smile. "Nice job. But what about your column?"

Pleased with her accomplishments, Malinda dusted her palms together, then pulled out the chair. "I was just getting ready to begin when I noticed that pitiful plant. Do you ever water it?"

Jack looked at the plant and wondered how long it had been there. "Mrs. O'Grady took care of those things," he mumbled.

Malinda smiled knowingly. "I see. Well, since she's gone, I guess you'll have to see to it yourself. Water at least once a week. Fertilize once a month. And make sure it gets plenty of sunlight."

She whipped out a piece of typing paper, fed it into the typewriter, then glanced up at him. "Was there something else?"

Jack just shook his head. "No. Nothing," he said as he backed from the room. "I just came in to tell you the boys and I are going outside to play in the snow."

Malinda waggled four fingers at him. "Well, have fun. Oh, and Jack," she called after him.

He stuck his head back in the doorway. "What?"

She smiled sweetly. "Be sure and have the boys wear their rubbers."

Jack closed the door behind him, took two steps and jerked to a stop. Still reeling from the whirlwind of changes in his study, it suddenly dawned on him what Malinda had just said.

Rubbers? he repeated to himself in disbelief. What the hell did she mean by telling him to be sure the boys wore their rubbers? How could she—Suddenly it dawned on him that she meant the *shoe* protector types and not... Jack gave a long, relieved sigh.

It wasn't as if he'd done it on purpose. The boys had chosen the spot for the snowman. It wasn't *his* fault they'd picked the area right outside the study window. And it wasn't *his* fault he had a bird's-eye view of Malinda working at his desk.

For long stretches of time she merely sat, her back rigid, staring off into space, the index finger of one hand tapping thoughtfully at her chin. Then she'd drop her hands to the keyboard and her fingers would fairly fly over the keys. When inspiration had obviously run its course, she'd stop, read what she'd typed, give the paper a satisfied nod, then stare off into space again.

The pattern was irritating as hell. Jack couldn't decide *why* it was irritating, it just was. He watched for a moment during the staring stage, wondering what on earth the woman could be thinking about so hard. After all, it was just manners she was writing. It wasn't as if she were penning the great American novel.

The longer he watched the more irritated he became. He finally decided it was her posture. She never slouched, stooped or relaxed her spine for a minute. Even when she thought no one was looking. Who could be that perfect all the time? Sure as hell not him, he thought and intentionally hunched his shoulders forward to prove the point.

"What are we going to use for eyes, Dad?"

Without moving his gaze from Malinda's rigid back, Jack waved a hand in the direction of the patio. "Go look in the grill and see if there's any charcoal left. A couple of chunks ought to do."

While Darren ran to check out the grill, Jack watched Malinda lift a hand to her hair, pluck out a pin and work a loose strand back into her bun. The movement was his undoing. He sucked in a breath and slowly blew it out through his teeth as he watched her breasts thrust forward, straining against the silk blouse, a result of the upward stretch of her arms.

He closed his eyes, conjuring up the image of her in his bed, minus the concealing blouse, her breasts bare but for a scrap of lace. Soft, rounded mounds a pearly white in the soft lamplight. Kissable, moldable. Groaning, he opened his eyes to stare at what he couldn't see, what the silk blouse so successfully disguised.

"Hey, Dad!"

Guiltily Jack ripped his gaze from the window and Malinda's voluptuous form. "What, Son?" he asked David.

"Can we use your fishing hat for the snowman?"

"Sure. It's hanging in the laundry room closet." For a moment Jack pretended interest in the snowman, but soon his gaze sought the study window.

She was typing again. Her back was arrow straight, her chin level with pressed-together knees. With her arms down, the shape of her breasts was concealed by her loose-fitting blouse. The hell of it was, he couldn't decide which made him madder. The fact that her posture was so erect, or the fact that he could no longer make out the rounded fullness of her breasts.

His breath started coming in shorter, angrier bursts, his nostrils flaring with each vaporous puff. *What is it with this woman?* he demanded of himself. He shouldn't care if she was in the house working her little fanny off while he and the boys were out playing in the snow. That was *her* problem, not his. And he shouldn't care whether her back ached from holding that ramrod-straight posture from dawn until dusk. It was *her* back, not his. But, damn it, it *did* make him mad, and he'd had about all he could take.

He spun around and headed for the back door, his jaw set and his fists clenched.

"Hey, Dad! Where're you going?" Jack, Jr., yelled.

"To the house," he shouted over his shoulder. "Keep an eye on your brothers."

He didn't slow down until he reached his bedroom. At his dresser he stopped and yanked open the bottom drawer. He jerked out a faded sweat suit, then slammed the drawer closed only to open it again and dig out a pair of athletic socks.

Moving on anger alone, he stomped to the study, flung open the door and tossed the pile of clothing onto the desk.

"Change your clothes. You're coming outside."

Malinda glanced up, startled. "What?"

"I said, change your clothes," he repeated, and planted his hands on his hips, daring her to defy him. "You're coming outside with us to play in the snow."

"But—"

"No buts."

Her chin lifted a fraction higher and he saw the obstinate glint appear in her eyes. He lowered his own chin and glowered at her through narrowed eyes. "If necessary, I can help you change."

Malinda swallowed hard, knowing the man was probably crass enough to make good his threat. Angrily she scraped the clothes onto her lap. "That won't be necessary. But I really don't see the purpose—"

"Ten minutes," he warned, his index finger aimed at her nose. "If you aren't outside, I'll be back."

Feeling like a complete fool, ten minutes later Malinda stepped out the back door, her feet swimming in a pair of rubbers three times her shoe size. She wore Jack's sweat suit and a ragged down jacket she'd found in the laundry room closet. The only clothing she could call her own was her bra and panties and a sensible pair of wool gloves she'd dug out of her purse.

Before she had a chance to tell the man just exactly what she thought of his overbearing attitude, a snowball caught her on the shoulder and exploded, pelting her face with snow.

"Oh-h-h-h," she screeched in an outraged voice. "You despicable fiend!" Without thinking, she bent and scooped a handful of snow and threw it at Jack's smug smile. He ducked and the snow hit the driveway with an ineffectual splat.

That only fed Malinda's fury. She scooped snow with both hands and let it fly, then scooped again, not even bothering to see if she'd hit her target. A snowball caught her on the collar and slid beneath her jacket. The bite of ice sliding down her back stole her breath and drew her to her toes. Tugging at the hem of the heavy jacket, she danced around, trying to shake out the freezing snow.

Squeals of delight came from the direction of the driveway. Perched on the hood of the Blazer, the four Brannan boys cheered their father on. Malinda stopped dancing long enough to glare at them. Instantly they became choirboys, hands folded between knees and wearing the most angelic expressions. They didn't fool Malinda for a minute. She knew they were enjoying this—and at her expense.

Out of the corner of her eye she glimpsed the snow shovel, lying forgotten on the patio. Inspiration struck. But so did Aunt Hattie.

No matter what the circumstances, a young woman should always conduct herself in a ladylike manner.

Malinda's hands froze only inches from the shovel, her gaze riveted on the tempting tool. "Just this once, Aunt Hattie," she whispered in desperation. "Please, just this once."

"What did you say, Miss Prim? I couldn't hear you," Jack yelled to her before doubling over in laughter again.

That did it! Malinda clamped her hands around the shovel's handle and stood.

Two wrongs do not make a right.

"Not this time, Aunt Hattie," she grated through clenched teeth. With one mighty stab of her foot, she sunk the blade into a drift and filled it with snow. Slowly she turned to face Jack, her eyes breathing fire and revenge.

Holding out his hands, he took a step backward, laughing. "I was only fooling, Malinda. A little fun, you know?" Another step back and his heel caught on the edge of the driveway concealed by a drift and he toppled backward, his arms flailing the air in an attempt to catch his balance. When he hit the ground, Malinda was on him, dumping the shovel of snow onto his face.

Still laughing, blinded by the snow, Jack made a wild grab for her. His fingers cinched her ankle. One tug and he had her stretched out on top of him in an unladylike sprawl.

The fall knocked the shovel from Malinda's hands and the breath from her lungs. She lay there a moment, stunned. Her hands, extended in a natural reflex to break her fall, were penned between their bodies and her face was buried between his shoulder and his neck.

As she struggled to breathe again, her ears rang, obliterating all other sound. But she could feel. At first only his laughter—vibrations against her breasts. And his breath—short, chuckling blasts at her ear. Then gradually she became aware of more intense sensations. The pressure of his thighs squeezing her right leg. The gentle swell of his manhood snuggled tight against her abdomen. And heavens! Was that his hands, cupping her rear end?

Mortified by the intimacy of their position, she pushed hard against his chest, grabbing at air to fill her starving lungs while levering her body upward until she could see his face.

Blue eyes wide with alarm met Jack's laughing brown ones. That frightened doe look of hers melted the smile right off his face. He couldn't have resisted even if he'd wanted to. Catching her reddened cheeks between the palms of his hands, he lifted his head until his lips met hers.

Cold. That was the first sensation that registered, followed quickly by a softness and a taste beyond description. He felt her fingers claw at the fabric of his jacket... but her face never budged an inch.

Emboldened by the knowledge that she was obviously as intrigued by this as he, Jack deepened the kiss, pushing against her full lips to trace their inner softness with his tongue. Fingers that once framed her face fanned back to capture her head, bringing her mouth more fully over his. Her breath became his, and his, hers.

Fire. Surrounded by snow and ice, he discovered a heat so intense it flashed through his body in a matter of seconds and burned all the way to his soul. Forgetting everything but the intense pleasure of the moment, he hooked a leg over hers and rolled.

"Way to go, Dad! You got her now!"

His son's voice reminded Jack that, unfortunately, he and Malinda were not alone. Catching her lower lip between his own, he slowly drew on it, ending the kiss.

"Yeah, but what do I do now that I've got her?" The question was directed at his son, but his gaze was riveted on Malinda's face. Her lips were swollen, her cheeks flushed a healthy red, but it was her eyes that held him. Both desire and confusion were reflected there. He'd suspected that a sensual woman lay hidden beneath the ladylike facade, but judging by the look on her face and the scared-rabbit pounding of her heart against his chest, he knew she hadn't a clue.

Malinda sat at the desk, her work spread beneath her propped elbows, staring off into space. Her mind was a thousand miles away—or at least half the length of the Brannans' house.

Where is he? What's he doing? she wondered. *Am I as much on his mind as he is on mine?*

She placed the tip of her index finger against her lower lip and slowly traced its shape. Closing her eyes, she gave herself up to the memory of Jack's kiss. Spirals of desire flooded her, turning her insides to warm honey. The kiss was so like the man. Strong, earthy, passionate, with just a touch of gentleness. Never in her life had she experienced a kiss like that. *Wonder if the kiss affected him the same way?*

She flipped her eyes open with a start. *You idiot,* she told herself and forced herself to pick up a letter from the desk. *Dumb, naive, inexperienced idiot,* she continued to admonish as she straightened the letter's folds. A man like Jack Brannan had probably kissed a million women in his lifetime and never thought twice about any one of them. So why did she think she was so special? If anything, the man was probably off having a good laugh over the entire matter.

The thought made her face burn in humiliation. Aunt Hattie was right—men couldn't be trusted. She'd do well to remember that in the future. In the meantime, she didn't have time for silly daydreams. She had work to do, a column to write. She gave the letter a firm snap and focused her attention on the message written there.

Dear Miss Prim,

I'm sixteen and madly in love with a guy in my biology class. Unfortunately he doesn't know I exist. What I want to know is this: Would it be okay for me to call and ask him for a date? My mom says no. What do you say? She says she'll go along with your decision.

The letter was simply signed "Desperate."

As was her pattern, Malinda tried to imagine what reply Aunt Hattie would give the teenager. She didn't have to think long. The answer was obvious. Hadn't Malinda heard the same sermon preached almost daily throughout her teenage years?

She placed the letter beside the typewriter and began to type.

Dear Desperate,

Although I understand your plight, I agree with your mother. A young lady should never call a young man and ask him for a date. The young man should do the asking.

To make him aware of your presence, you might consider teaming up with him on a special class project, or perhaps ask his opinion on a matter you've discussed in class.

Good luck!

"That's the biggest bunch of bull I've ever heard in my life!"

Malinda jumped at the sound of Jack's voice. Unaware he'd even entered the study, she was shocked when she turned to find him standing directly behind her, reading over her shoulder. Although he'd changed his wet clothes, his attire was much the same—faded jeans and a ragged sweatshirt. He looked good . . . too good.

Reminding herself of her pledge to keep a safe distance, she glanced back at the paper in the typewriter. "What's bull?"

Jack waved a hand at the paper. "All that! What's wrong with the girl calling the guy if she wants to?"

"It's just not done."

Jack grabbed a straight-back chair and pulled it along-side Malinda's, then straddled it. "Says who?"

With him so close, Malinda found it hard to concentrate.

"Well—Aunt Hattie for one. She—"

"Who the hell is Aunt Hattie?"

"Agatha Prim. The creator of this column and my aunt," Malinda replied defensively.

"Prim?" he repeated. He cocked his head toward her and tried not to smile. "Kind of fits, doesn't it?"

Although she knew he was right, Malinda's cheeks burned in humiliation. She hated the name "Miss Prim." No one had dared call Aunt Hattie by her given name. They'd all called her Miss Prim, which was just fine considering that was her name. The rub had come after her death, when Malinda had taken over the column and people had started calling her that same name.

Guilt stabbed at her at the traitorous thought, for Aunt Hattie had always taken great pride in her name as well as her reputation. Remembering this, Malinda lifted her chin proudly. "Yes, it does fit. Aunt Hattie was very much the lady."

Jack sensed he'd hit a nerve. Common sense told him to back off, but curiosity made him dig a little deeper.

"If your aunt's the originator of this column, how come you're writing it?"

Malinda drew in a deep breath. "It's a long and boring story. I'm sure you don't want to hear it."

Crossing his arms over the chair's back, Jack settled his chin on his forearm. "Sure I do."

Malinda eyed him a moment, then decided he was serious. Sighing, she folded her hands in her lap. "Aunt Hattie started the column about twenty years ago and over the years people began to rely on her advice. They would write and ask about certain problems they had concerning proper etiquette and she would print her replies in her column.

"When she first got sick, she fretted so. Who would take over for her, who would people turn to when they needed advice?" She shrugged. "So I started helping her. Before long I was writing the column myself. She seemed to rest easier knowing her work was being continued. After her death, I just kept writing."

"How do you come up with the answers to the questions?"

"For the most part, I rely on Aunt Hattie's training. She raised me," she said in explanation. "When I'm not sure about something, I have a stack of reference books I turn to."

"Do you always agree with the advice you give?"

His questions were beginning to get on her nerves. Wishing she could avoid this one in particular, she gave each of her sleeves' cuffs a firm snap. "Whether or not I agree isn't important. It's whether or not the advice is correct."

"Correct in whose mind?"

"The authorities on the subject, of course."

"And who are the authorities?"

Malinda fairly squirmed in her chair. "The people who write the etiquette books, I guess," she finally blurted out. "I don't know." Hoping to put an end to the inquisition, she looked away.

A heavy silence followed. Unfortunately his silence made her as uneasy as his questions. She stole a glance his way only to find him sitting, his chin resting on his forearms, watching her. When her gaze met his, he smiled that irresistible grin she'd already grown to dread.

"You are one frustrated woman."

Malinda's mouth dropped open. "What!" she gasped.

"You're frustrated. You live by some archaic set of standards you don't even agree with and you're mad because you feel you have to."

"That is simply not true!"

"It is and I can prove it." He pushed out of the chair, spun it around to face Malinda and sat back down. He leaned forward, propping his forearms on his knees, placing his face less than a foot from hers. "Touch me," he said.

Shocked by his request, Malinda attempted to scoot her chair away from him. Penned by the desk on one side and Jack on the other, the only direction she could go was backward. Jack thwarted that move with one well-placed foot behind the chair's leg.

"Go ahead," he encouraged. "Touch me."

Malinda locked her hands into a tight fist on her lap, lifted her chin and refused to look at him. "I don't want to touch you."

"Yes, you do." He inched closer until his knees brushed hers, nearly suffocating her with his nearness. "You want to know how I know? Every time I get near you, you tense up and you grab something or you twist your hands up in knots so you won't be tempted to touch me."

Though she would have preferred to deny it, the truth in the statement made Malinda's cheeks burn in embarrassment. Hoping to hide this fact from him, she dropped her chin and focused on her lap. Immediately her eyes filled with tears. The proof was right there before her—fingers twisted together so tight the knuckles glowed a pearly white.

"It's okay to touch people, Malinda," he said softly. He reached out and took her hands in his. Slowly he began to untwine her fingers. The effect was devastating. With the release of each one, Malinda felt another portion of her resistance melt away.

In his touch she discovered a strength bridled by a gentleness that drew fresh tears to her eyes. Though her mind screamed for him to stop, emotion clogged her throat, robbing her of speech.

When the last finger was lifted, then freed, she attempted to pull away but he tightened his grip. He continued to hold one hand but drew the other to his face, drawing her gaze there, as well.

Flattening her palm against his cheek, he smiled. The play of facial muscles rippled beneath her trembling fingers. Slowly she shifted her gaze from their joined hands to his eyes. "It *is* soft," she whispered.

"What's soft, Malinda?"

"Your beard."

Chuckling, he rubbed her hand beneath his and she winced, then laughed. She shook his hand loose and smoothed her hand down his cheek, then back up. "Amazing," she said, returning her hand to her lap. "When I rub one way it's soft and the other it's as coarse as sandpaper."

"Only because I need a shave." Jack cocked his head and lifted a brow at her. "That wasn't so bad, was it?"

Malinda dipped her head, hiding her flushed cheeks from him.

"Don't worry," he promised with a pat on her knee. "It'll get easier. You'll see." He leaned over as he rose and touched his lips to her cheek. "Night, Malinda."

Five

———

"**W**ell, what do you say? Will you take us on?"

The rejection speech was there, in her head. Malinda knew this because she'd stayed awake half the night formulating it and practicing it. But for some reason the words wouldn't come.

Knowing how weak-kneed she was in the face of adversity—specifically Jack Brannan's persuasive charm—she'd prepared for this confrontation the night before, giving herself every possible edge. She'd handwashed her undergarments—for who could present a confident front wearing day-old panties—and shampooed her hair. Of course her skirt and blouse were the same ones she'd donned Friday afternoon prior to arriving at the Brannans'. And the only makeup she wore consisted of a touch of lip gloss and a dab of pressed powder from her compact, the only cosmetic items she carried in her purse. But she'd done her best.

One look at Jack across the breakfast table and she knew her best wasn't going to be good enough. Fresh from the shower, he wore what seemed to be his standard attire—faded jeans and a ragged sweatshirt. Ordinarily such casual dress on a man would leave her unimpressed.

But not when worn by Jack. The jeans accentuated muscled thighs and slim hips. The sweatshirt—sleeves shoved to the elbows—hugged a chest Malinda feared she could recognize blindfolded. Add to that a freshly shaven face, hair still damp from a shower and a smile that would charm the skin off a snake, and Malinda knew without a doubt she didn't stand a chance.

Armed with looks, charm, a childhood history that would bring tears to Captain Hook's eyes, and four of the neediest children she'd ever seen, Jack had the deck stacked in his favor.

A woman's strength lies in her reputation.

Malinda felt like throwing open the window and screaming at the top of her lungs. Why couldn't Aunt Hattie, just this once, mind her own business? Malinda *knew* she shouldn't accept his offer of employment. Hadn't she stayed up half the night arriving at that same conclusion? The problem was she *wanted* to accept it. She knew it was insane, considering all that had occurred in the forty-eight hours she'd spent with the Brannans.

The three oldest boys were hellions. Their house was a disorganized mess. And their father, she feared, was a womanizer of the worst kind. Yet Malinda ached to give the boys the love and guidance they needed to develop into proper little gentlemen, and whip the household into shape.

And upon reflection, she had to admit the experience hadn't been *all* bad. She'd never had a snowball fight in her life—Aunt Hattie didn't approve of such nonsense—and she'd never had a man melt her bones with a simple kiss.

Malinda...

A shiver chased down Malinda's spine. Aunt Hattie had always had a way of saying her name with just enough inflection on the last syllable to throw Malinda into a guilt trip that lasted a week. Even from the grave her voice held that same power.

Reluctantly Malinda murmured to Jack, "I'm sorry, but I really can't take the job."

"Can't, or won't?"

Malinda nearly groaned. Why couldn't the man accept a simple no? Why did he have to always press? Thankfully the phone rang, saving her from having to justify her decision.

Jack rocked his chair back on two legs and snagged the receiver from the wall unit. "Brannan," he said in a clipped voice. he listened a moment, then dropped his forehead against his palm, rubbing at the worry lines that had instantly appeared. "How bad is it?" After another long pause, he sighed deeply and said, "No, I need to be there. I'll call you back as soon as I make the flight arrangements."

He dropped the receiver back onto the cradle and the chair to all four legs. "That was Jim McIntire, my site supervisor," he said in explanation. "Part of the roof collapsed on the office complex I'm building in Chicago. I've got to get back up there as quick as I can."

Malinda's thoughts immediately flew to the children who were still sleeping. "What about the boys?"

Frowning, Jack tunneled his fingers through his hair. "They'll have to go with me."

"But who will take care of them?"

"Most hotels offer baby-sitting services. If not, I'll contact an agency once we get there."

The thought of the boys being left in a hotel room with some stranger made her stomach muscles tighten in reaction. Considering their treatment of her, the empathetic feelings were amazing, but she couldn't stop them any more than she could stop the snow from falling outside. "What about school?"

Jack shoved back his chair and stood, a frown building on his face. "They'll just have to miss." He strode to the sink and dumped his coffee down the drain.

Malinda rose, too, and followed him. "You can't do that."

Jack wheeled to face her, his face now flushed an angry red. "Don't tell me what I can and can't do." He strode past her, then turned back. "Do you think it's easy being a single parent? I'm busting my ass to give those kids everything I never had and trying to be both a mother and a father to them at the same time." He threw up his hands in a hopeless gesture. "And so what if they miss a couple of days of school? It isn't as if I have any other option."

Malinda stiffened her spine and swallowed hard while memories of her own childhood twisted her heart. Knowing full well she would regret this, she replied in a calm voice, "Yes you do."

"What?" he demanded, his voice full of frustration.

"I'll stay with them."

For a moment Jack just stared at her. Then a broad grin slowly spread across his face. "You will?"

Malinda lifted her chin and pursed her lips. "I said I would, didn't I?"

The words were hardly out of her mouth before he was crossing the room, whooping loudly and wearing a look that Malinda feared meant she was about to be gathered up in his arms and spun around the room. She held out one hand to stop him.

"I'll stay until you return from Chicago," she said firmly. "Not a minute longer. So you better start looking for another housekeeper."

Jack pushed the security card into the slot, twisted the handle and shouldered open the door to his motel room. Shrugging out of his coat, he crossed the room to the phone where the message light blinked an impatient red.

Please, no more bad news, he begged as he punched the number for the front desk. "Brannan, room 114. Do you have a message for me?"

"Yes, sir. Several. Your secretary in Oklahoma City wants you to call her as soon as possible, and a Mr. Phipps with the city's inspection department called several times. He said it's urgent."

After jotting down Phipps's phone number, Jack mumbled a thanks, depressed the plunger, then quickly released it and punched in his office number. Phipps could wait. His secretary couldn't. More than likely she was calling to let him know that all hell had broken loose on the home front. Specifically, Malinda Compton had changed her mind about keeping the boys.

Impatiently he switched the phone to the opposite ear. He knew he should have brought the boys with him.

"Brannan Construction. This is Liz."

As always, his secretary's chipper voice worked like a balm on his frazzled nerves. "It is?" he teased.

"Last time I looked in a mirror. How's Chicago?"

"A mess. How are things there?"

"Snow's melting and the weatherman's predicting a high of sixty tomorrow."

"That's Oklahoma for you."

Liz laughed. "I didn't call to discuss Oklahoma's unpredictable weather. I called to let you know I contacted the insurance adjuster. He'll meet you at the construction site at eight in the morning. Don't be late. The guy sounds like a bear."

"They all are. Anything else?"

"Nope. All's clear here."

Jack knitted his forehead into a frown, then rubbed at it. "No messages from home?"

"Not a word."

"You're sure?" he asked doubtfully.

"Positive."

"Well, call if you need me."

"Will do, boss."

Jack replaced the receiver and stretched out on the bed. No messages from home. He couldn't believe it. Working a toe against the opposite heel, he pushed off his boots while he alternately built and discarded different scenarios of the situation at home. Either Malinda had put the fear of God in his sons, he finally decided, or the boys had really built that funeral pyre and burned her at the stake, in which case she couldn't call for help.

Chuckling, he tucked his hands behind his head and lay back, silently hoping it was the former, not the latter. With his hands pillowed behind his head, he closed his eyes for the first time in more than twenty-four hours and willed his muscles to relax. He'd rest for just a minute, he promised himself, then he'd call home and check on the... Sleep came before he completed the thought.

Hours later he jerked awake. Without analyzing the depressed feeling that weighed on him, he knew its origin. He'd been dreaming again. The same dreams that had haunted him most of his life.

He stared at the shadowed wall opposite him, watching it change from dull gray to vibrant red to soothing blue, then back to gray, the handiwork of the motel's marquee out front.

So much like his life, he thought as he watched the colors bleed from one to the next. From dismal shadows to bright color, the segmented years of his life marched through his mind. Shadowed memories of being shuttled from foster home to foster home, never having roots or family or any sense of belonging. He'd survived, but not without emotional scars he still fought to hide.

Then there had come color. Laurel. Full of laughter and fun. God, how he had loved her. But then, as he had discovered too late, so had every other man in town. And she'd shared.

The tightness in his chest told him the memory still hurt, and he shoved it away. From darkness to light and back to darkness. No, not total darkness, he thought, his hands tightening into fists against the bedspread. His sons. They were the color in his life now. In them he had discovered that sense of belonging, that sense of being needed and wanted that had escaped him most of his life. And as much as he needed them, he knew they needed their father and he wouldn't let them down. Not like his parents had let him down.

He squinted an eye at his watch and noted the time. Damn! he thought as he jerked upright. Almost ten o'clock. But maybe if he was lucky they'd still be up and he could talk to them.

He picked up the phone and dialed.

"Brannan residence."

He couldn't help smiling at the formal tone in Malinda's voice. Even at this hour and over the phone no less, Miss Prim was in full form. "It's Jack. How's it going?"

"Fine. How is Chicago?"

He lay back down, cupping one hand behind his head. "Cold."

Malinda's answering laugh had a soothing ring to it. The sound washed over him, taking the last kinks out of his tensed muscles.

"Did you resolve your problem with the roof?" she asked.

"No, but I'm working on it. Are the boys in bed?"

"Yes, and hopefully asleep."

He quickly squelched his disappointment at not getting to talk to them. "Are you making out all right? I mean with your work schedule and all?"

"Yes, everything's fine. This morning after we dropped the boys off at school, Patrick and I went to the shop. Then when school was out, they all came to the shop and worked on their homework until it was time to go home."

"Are they giving you any trouble?"

"Not a bit. We're getting along great."

Puzzled by the miraculous change in his sons' behavior, Jack frowned at the receiver. He knew he should be relieved that all was going well, but for some strange reason he wasn't. "Maybe I ought to cancel that classified ad I asked my secretary to run and talk you into staying on."

"Oh, I don't know . . ."

The doubt in her voice soothed his battered ego—for the moment. "Well, if the boys give you any trouble or if you need anything, call my secretary. She'll know how to contact me during the day or you can reach me at the motel at night."

"I'm sure we'll be fine."

Jack toyed with the phone cord, searching for something to say, a reason to remain on the line and maintain that link with home. An excuse to hear the sound of Malinda's voice. Unfortunately he came up empty-handed. "Well...I guess I better let you go. If you need anything—"

"Yes, I know. Call your secretary."

The laughter in her voice grated against his already pent-up frustrations. He wanted to be home, damn it. Building snowmen with his kids and drinking hot chocolate. And, yes, damn it, snuggling up next to Malinda in front of a blazing fire and melting a little more of that starch from her spine. Not shut up in some nondescript motel room with only himself for company.

Frustrated by his responsibilities to his job and his own warring emotions, he mumbled a goodbye and hung up the phone. He glared at the constantly changing lights on the far wall, the corners of his mouth pulled down in a frown.

It was hell not to feel needed.

Eight hundred miles away Malinda dropped the receiver back onto the wall unit in the kitchen and at the same time uncrossed the fingers she still held behind her back. Lying had never come easily.

Shrugging away the untruths as necessary, considering the problems Jack already had to deal with, she scooped a pile of dirty clothes from the floor, crossed to the laundry room and stuffed it unceremoniously into the washing machine. She paused for a moment, a hand pressed at the dull ache in her lower back, before she stretched to switch on the machine.

How do working mothers manage everything? she wondered as she shuffled wearily back to the kitchen where the dinner dishes still waited by the sink. After little more than twenty-four hours, she was exhausted and ready to throw in the towel.

She groaned as she pulled open the door to the dishwasher, remembering the boldness of her lies to Jack. "Everything is just fine," she said, mimicking her earlier bravado to the boys' father. "Fine, my foot," she muttered testily. Taking a nylon scrubber from the rack beneath the sink, she began to rub at the circles of dried milk on the glasses that lined the counter.

If everything was fine, why did the back of her neck feel like someone had rammed a three-inch steel pipe down its length? And why did she feel as if she needed to spend an hour with a child psychologist to resolve her inadequacies in dealing with the Brannan boys?

And why, she asked herself as she swiped the back of a soapy hand beneath her eyes, did she have this overpowering need to sit down and have a good cry?

Squaring her shoulders, she blinked back the tears and scrubbed harder at the circles of dried milk. "Because you're tired," she lectured in a firm voice. "Because you're not accustomed to caring for a house this size and keeping up with four rambunctious boys."

She sniffed and picked up a plate. "And you *are* inadequate when it comes to dealing with children who are so obviously starved for attention because—" She stopped and rested her wrists against the sink's edge as she lifted her gaze to meet her reflection in the kitchen window. The eyes that stared back at her were large and haunted. "Because," she repeated, her voice breaking with emotion, "you know how it feels to be left with strangers."

Blinded by the tears that welled in her eyes, she quickly slipped the plate into the bottom rack of the dishwasher. Snatching the dish towel from the counter, she wiped at first her hands, then her eyes, as she turned her back on the dirty dishes. In the den she slumped to the couch, the memories of her own childhood like a heavy weight on her shoulders, pushing her down.

Yes, she knew well how it was to be left with strangers. Like Jack Brannan's, her father's business had required travel. Not only within the United States, but around the world, as well.

And when his business had grown, he had decided it prudent for him to live overseas. He had included his wife in that decision to move. Unfortunately he hadn't included his daughter. Thinking it in her best interest to remain in the States, he had left Malinda in the care of a continuing series of nannies and housekeepers while he and his wife had lived in the Middle East.

Like the Brannan boys, Malinda had rebelled. Frustrated by their daughter's continued defiance, in desperation the Comptons had parked Malinda in the care of a maiden aunt. Aunt Hattie. Malinda smiled through her tears at the memory.

A sixty-year-old spinster taking on a rebellious eight-year-old. In retrospect Malinda wondered why Aunt Hattie had ever agreed to the arrangement. But agree she had, and the decision had changed Malinda's life dramatically.

She dabbed at her eyes with the dish towel, remembering. Separated by more than two generations, they'd had their share of differences. But through it all Aunt Hattie had remained unflappable. Granted, her ideas about a young woman's behavior had been antiquated to Malinda's young mind, and her constant quoting of truisms grating to say the least. But she had been there, offering a home and security, and for that Malinda would always be grateful.

And she would be there for Jack's children, she thought with renewed fervor as she pushed to her feet and headed back to the kitchen and the pile of dirty dishes. Maybe not always. But for now. Because she, of all people, understood their insecurities, their fears.

"Isn't tonight your Cub Scout pack meeting?"

Slouched in his chair, Jack, Jr., hunched lower over his bowl and shoveled another spoonful of cereal into his mouth. "Yeah, but I'm not going."

In the process of spooning another mouthful of oatmeal to Patrick, Malinda paused and glanced over her shoulder. "Sit up straight in your chair, please, and don't talk with food in your mouth," she said automatically before asking, "Why not?"

"'Cause they're stupid."

Darren chimed in, "And 'cause it's his turn to take refreshments." The twins burst out laughing. Jack, Jr., silenced them with one killing glance.

Not understanding what lay behind the discussion, Malinda offered softly, "If it's the refreshments you're worried about, Jack, we can take care of that. What do you usually take when it's your turn?"

His spoon hit his bowl with a loud clunk. "A dumb bag of cookies." With that he shoved away from the table and stormed from the room.

Surprised by his angry exit, Malinda looked to Darren for an explanation. "What was that all about?"

Darren scrunched up his mouth and shrugged. "All the other kids' moms make neat snacks like gingerbread men and popcorn balls and stuff. They hate it when it's Jack's turn 'cause he always brings boring store-bought cookies."

Malinda leaned back in her chair, unknowingly pulling the spoon farther away from the already straining Patrick. *So that's it,* she thought sadly. He was embarrassed.

Deep in thought, she swung the spoon back and forth while Patrick made unsuccessful lunges at it, his mouth open.

Cecile's son, Jared, was close to Jack, Jr.'s, age. Malinda had spent enough time with her business partner's family to know her friend's children fairly well, so she had a vague idea of an eight-year-old boy's likes and dislikes...and also how cruel their teasing could be.

Two months ago she'd attended Jared's birthday party. Cecile had baked the cake, a huge monstrosity of a thing that looked like some kind of monster to Malinda, but was in fact, she'd been informed, a Teenage Mutant Ninja Turtle. Malinda had nearly gagged at the icing's putrid green color. The children had loved it.

Much to Patrick's dismay, Malinda dropped the spoon back into the bowl of oatmeal, reached for the wall phone and dialed her business partner's number.

"Cecile?" she said in a clipped voice. "Malinda. Don't ask questions, just listen. I only have a minute. I need the recipe for that hideous cake you baked for Jared's birthday party."

After six days of arguing with subcontractors, fighting his way through the City of Chicago's building inspector's bureaucratic red tape and tossing and turning in a strange bed, Jack was home. A soldier returning from war couldn't have felt any more jubilant.

He pushed open the back door and stepped into the kitchen. Immediately the weariness and the tension from the trip melted away. Across the room, Malinda stood at the sink, her back to him, a pile of freshly peeled potatoes at her right. She wore a dress—silk, judging by the glossy fabric—and an apron tied at her waist. An apron! Jack stifled a laugh. The last woman he'd seen wear an apron was Mrs. Lightfoot, one of his foster mothers, and that had been more than fifteen years ago.

He watched for a moment, fascinated, as she dropped a potato onto the pile then selected another from the bottom of the sink to peel. Her movements were fluid, natural, with no wasted motion. She was a woman who obviously knew her way around a kitchen.

A sense of rightness struck him. *This is how life should be,* he thought. A man comes home after a hard day's work to find his wife in the kitchen, cooking his dinner.

His life had never been like that with Laurel. When he'd come home after a hard day, he'd usually find a sitter with the kids, take-out pizza growing cold on the kitchen table and a note from Laurel telling him she'd be home late. Not the kind of life he'd envisioned for himself at all.

The sound of his sons' voices raised in an argument came from the den. Jack opened his mouth to tell them to cool it, but before he could make a sound Malinda called out, "Disagreements can be settled without raising your voices, boys."

Instantly the yelling ceased. Jack swallowed his own warning to the boys and stared at Malinda's back in disbelief. How had she done that?

The oven timer buzzed and Malinda dropped the potato she'd been scraping into the sink. Taking a hot pad from the counter, she pulled open the oven door. Mouthwatering aromas immediately filled the room. Jack breathed deeply, assimilating and sorting each scent. Meat loaf and, if memory served him right, peach cobbler. After a week of eating his food out of disposable containers, he thought he'd died and gone to heaven.

Evidently Malinda hadn't heard his entrance because she continued to hum an accompaniment to the classical music playing from the intercom's speaker as she pulled the steaming dishes from the oven. Quitely he closed the door behind him and tiptoed across the room.

At her back he stopped and leaned his head over her shoulder, breathing deeply of the mouth-watering smells. "And she can cook," he said half to himself.

Malinda stifled a scream and juggled the hot dish, struggling not to burn herself as she shoved it onto the countertop. "Heavens!" she said, wheeling around to face him. With only scant inches between them, she pressed a hand against his chest to still the momentum of her turn. "You nearly scared the life out of me," she said breathlessly, aware of where her hand rested but unable to move it.

Jack only grinned. "Sorry." He closed his fingers around hers and pulled her hand above her head, turning her in a slow pirouette. With her at his side and both of them now facing the counter, he dropped his hand to encircle her waist.

The gesture was casual, easy. The posture a man might share with his wife. Over the past week, Malinda had shared other such moments with Jack, and though they had lacked the physical contact, they were no less intimate. Nightly phone calls during which they discussed their day. Conversations concerning the children's activities and welfare. Even the mundane tasks of cleaning his house, doing his laundry and caring for his children had drawn her closer to him.

Malinda freeze-framed the fantasy that was building in her mind before it bloomed out of control. Jack Brannan was *not* her husband and this was *not* her home. He was her employer, a man at ease with himself and the world.

And Malinda was anything but at ease. Every muscle in her body was tense and every nerve on red alert. The woman in her wanted nothing more than to respond to his openness—wrap an arm at his waist and lean into the warmth of that sideways hug. But years of living with Aunt Hattie, where physical displays of emotion were taboo, made her suppress that urge and clasp her hands together at her waist instead.

Immediately she regretted the move, remembering Jack's lecture on touching. Hoping he hadn't noticed the telling action, she quickly dropped her hands to her sides just as he dipped his head over the peach cobbler and sniffed.

"Dinner?" he asked.

"Dessert. The meat loaf—"

"Daddy!" Three voices screamed in unison.

Jack spun around, took two ground-eating steps and spread out his arms, catching his three oldest sons in a giant bear hug. They squealed in delight as their sneakers left the floor.

From her position by the oven, Malinda watched. It was all she could do to keep from flying across the room and becoming a part of that hug.

How many times as a child had she dreamed of such a homecoming for herself? In her dream her dad would come home and she'd race across the room and into his waiting arms. He'd laugh, hugging her tight against his chest, or maybe toss her high in the air and tell her how much he'd missed her while he'd been gone.

She swallowed back the emotional lump that rose with the vision. Dreams. With parents who lived halfway around the world, dreams were all she'd had as a child.

Patrick toddled up and wrapped his arms around his dad's knees, babbling, "Daddy, Daddy, Daddy." His determination to be a part of the excitement touched Malinda's heart. Crossing to the child, she swung him up in her arms. "Someone else wants to say hello," she said, smiling at Jack over the top of Patrick's tousled hair.

Jack eased the boys back to the floor and opened his arms. Patrick fell into them with an excited squeal, locking his arms tight around his dad's neck. Satisfied with the attention he'd received, he leaned back, cupping Jack's cheeks between his chubby hands. "Lindy needs a hug, too," he said in a matter-of-fact voice.

If there had been a rug on the floor, Malinda would have crawled under it.

Jack, his lips puckered by Patrick's hands, asked in a muffled voice, "And who's Lindy?"

Patrick withdrew one hand to point a stubby finger at Malinda.

"Lindy?" Jack repeated, his eyes teasing her.

Mortified by the child's announcement that she needed a hug, Malinda lifted a shoulder in what she hoped came across as a nonchalant shrug. "Patrick has a hard time pronouncing Malinda, so he shortened it to Lindy."

His eyes sparkling with amusement, Jack continued to look at her for a moment before turning back to Patrick. "And you think Lindy needs a hug, huh?"

Patrick's head bobbed up and down, his expression serious.

"Well, then—" Jack shifted Patrick to his hip and stretched an arm around Malinda's shoulders, pulling her to his side. "If you think Lindy needs a hug, it's a hug she'll get."

Though she'd known it was coming, the physical contact was no less shocking. Warmth, strength and, yes, even comfort. Each sensation, each emotion wrapped itself around her, filling in voids empty for too many years.

A second arm—much smaller than the first—wound itself around her neck. Thankful for the distraction, Malinda opened her hands in invitation and Patrick transferred himself to her arms.

Chuckling, Jack picked up his duffel bag from where he'd dropped it by the back door. "Patrick always has had a way with the women. When's dinner?" he asked as he passed by Malinda.

"In about thirty minutes. We were just discussing whose turn it is to set the table."

Jack stopped so quickly that Darren, who was trailing behind him, slammed into him. "The boys set the table?" he asked in surprise.

"Yes. Is that a problem?"

"No, I just didn't know they knew how."

"They didn't," Malinda replied. "But table setting is a part of all my etiquette classes. In my opinion, if a child knows what comprises a proper setting, he'll be more at ease in a formal situation." She nodded toward the refrigerator as she lowered Patrick to his feet. "I drew an example of a proper place setting and hung it on the refrigerator. If the boys forget, they refer to it."

Silent throughout her explanation, Jack rubbed a palm across the back of his neck and stole a glance at the sketch on the refrigerator. A minimum of five pieces of silverware were aligned beside the plate. His neck muscles tensed beneath his fingers.

In his opinion, a fork and a plate were the only tools necessary to eat. Oh, and maybe a knife if you were having a steak. Everything else was fluff, what people did to put on airs, to show off their superiority.

But the kids' teachers had said they were uncivilized heathens, he reminded himself. And if this is what it took for them to be accepted—well, then they'd learn to eat with an arsenal of equipment.

He took a deep breath and willed his muscles to relax. It didn't work. Change made him uncomfortable, always had.

Without saying a word, he turned and strode from the kitchen.

Six

And his sons' learning to set a table wasn't the only change Jack noted as he strode through the house on his way to his bedroom. The changes were subtle in one sense, monumental in another.

A wicker basket, one which he vaguely remembered putting out in the garage months ago, sat next to the couch, stuffed to the brim with toys that were usually scattered across the floor. The television set, which was turned on for morning cartoons and blared nonstop until bedtime, was concealed behind the wooden louvered doors of the entertainment center. And the game table, on most days camouflaged beneath an array of toys and games, was cleared of all but a few books.

Jack crossed to the table and picked up a textbook. Math. Third-grade math to be exact, and beside the book lay notebook paper, half-filled with his oldest son's familiar scrawl. Jack knew for a fact his son hated homework, especially math, and completed it only under duress. But from the looks of things, Jack, Jr., had been working on his assignment on his own and without the threatening presence of an adult hanging over his shoulder. Jack eased the book back to the table and headed for his bedroom.

A week, he reminded himself as he dropped his duffel bag to his bed. He'd only been gone a week and already Malinda had made dramatic alterations in both his home and his sons. The boys were studying, setting tables, cleaning up after themselves.

But Jack didn't like change. His marriage to Laurel had taught him that.

He stopped a moment, realizing the direction of his thoughts. Anger. Resentment. He could feel both rising within him. And the emotions were all too familiar.

And that's stupid, he thought with a shake of his head. He'd hired Malinda to take care of his kids and that's exactly what she'd done. And if she made a few changes around the house, who was he to complain? It wasn't as if she'd tried to change *him* in any way.

And besides, she was going home, he reminded himself. Tonight. Probably right after dinner. She'd made that clear before he'd left town.

So what am I getting so worked up about? he asked himself. *We made a deal and she's done a damn good job keeping her end of it.* Even so, a frown shored up between his brows as he shrugged out of his shirt.

He didn't want her to go home, he finally admitted as he dropped the shirt to the floor and pulled a clean one from his closet. He kind of liked having her around. Granted, she was a bit of a prude, but he could understand that, considering she'd been raised by an old maid. Over the past week, he'd learned that and a whole lot more about her during their nightly phone calls.

He dropped down on the bed, dangling the shirt by its collar between his spread legs. He'd enjoyed those phone calls. In fact, during the day, he'd catch himself watching the clock, anxious to get back to his room to make those calls. He'd needed that contact with home... with her. His frown deepened.

It had been a long time since he'd needed anyone—other than his sons, of course. He wasn't sure he liked the idea.

Shaking off the uncomfortable feeling, he pulled on the shirt. He had three buttons hooked before it hit him. His fingers poised at the fourth buttonhole, he slowly dipped his head and stared at the shirtfront. Not a wrinkle in it, and judging by the stiffness of the collar and in the cuffs, starch had been used.

A sense of déjà vu swept over him. Laurel had tried similar tactics. What had started with starched shirts quickly grew to three-piece suits, designer labels and a membership at the country club.

"Malinda!" he bellowed. He threw his closet door wide, looking for more evidence of her invasion into his privacy. It didn't take long. His entire closet had been rearranged. All his jeans were gone and his slacks had been pulled from the back of his closet to the front. His sports shirts had been separated from his dress shirts. His shoes were lined up in neat rows on the closet floor.

Sucking in an outraged breath, he yelled in a voice he knew from experience could be heard all the way to the kitchen, "Malinda! Get in here!"

Seconds later she appeared in the doorway, breathless, her cheeks still rosy from her work over the hot stove.

Seeing the angry flush on his face, Malinda asked uncertainly, "Is something wrong?"

"You're damned right something's wrong! Who ironed my shirt?"

"I did."

"Why?" he demanded.

"Well," she replied, perplexed by the absurdity of the question. "It was in the hamper with the dirty clothes, and when I did the children's laundry I did yours, as well."

Angrily he yanked the buttons from their holes. "I don't pay you to do my laundry. And I sure as hell don't pay you to stick your nose into my personal things."

The statement cut deep. So deep, Malinda had to struggle to conceal the hurt. No, he didn't pay her to do his laundry or to rearrange his personal items. He paid her to teach his sons manners and, for the past week, to see to their safety in his absence. She would do well to remember that in the future.

Lifting her chin a notch, she looked him square in the eye. "No, you don't pay me to do your laundry," she said trying hard to still the tremble in her voice. "I'm sorry if I overstepped my bounds."

The shirt now unbuttoned, Jack stripped it off, then, holding it aloft, shook it at her. "And I don't put starch in my shirts. Hell, I don't even iron my shirts."

Her eyes focused on the shirt, Malinda watched him wad it into a ball and throw it onto the bed...and rued the hours she'd spent ironing his clothes and organizing his closet. Time she should have spent working on her newspaper column, which was due on the editor's desk by eight the next morning.

His hands splayed at his hips, he continued to berate her. "Starched shirts are better suited on some five-dollar attorney," he said, jabbing a thumb at his chest to drive home his point. "Not on me."

Malinda laced her fingers together at her waist and stared at them, willing herself not to give in to the tears that pricked her eyes. "As I said, I'm sorry if I overstepped my bounds.'' She glanced up, but her gaze never made it any higher than his chest.

She'd seen Jack barechested before, but that had been at night. In his bed. And darkness had done a lot in concealing the muscled contours shadowed beneath the dark hair curling there. At the moment, his chest was swelled in anger and his left nipple throbbed with the angry cadence of his heartbeat.

She felt the heat creep up her neck and a more unsettling one spread throughout her abdomen. Appalled by her reaction, she wheeled around, turning her back to him. ''If we are to continue this discussion, I would appreciate it if you would please cover yourself.''

He made a sound, a cross somewhere between a snort and a laugh, before he replied, ''I'll just bet you would. But this is *my* house and *my* bedroom and I'll dress any damn way I please.''

''As you wish.'' She started for the bedroom door, her knees shaking uncontrollably. ''I'll pack my things and say goodbye to the boys.''

''Fine by me.''

The slam of the bathroom door behind Jack was followed by the soft click of the bedroom door as Malinda quietly left the room.

When Jack entered the kitchen, he was greeted by four sets of accusing eyes.

Immediately he took the defensive. ''So what's wrong with you guys?'' he asked.

''Malinda left.''

Jack met Darren's accusing look with a shrug. ''So? She agreed to stay until I got home. I'm home, so she's free to leave.''

''We didn't want her to leave.''

The last statement came from Jack, Jr., and the boy couldn't have shocked his father more if he'd just announced he'd decided to take up ballet.

"And you made her cry," David added. "Why'd you make her cry?"

Cry? Jack looked at his son in surprise. He hadn't known she'd cried. The thought that he was the cause of her tears made him feel about as low as a snake. He shoved back the guilt. It wasn't his fault she'd cried. *She* was the one who had stuck her nose where it didn't belong, and if you stuck your nose in other people's business you had to expect sometimes to get it bent.

Jack pulled out a chair at the kitchen table. "I didn't *make* her cry. That's just how women are. They're emotional." He shoved a place setting to the side in order to rest his forearms on the table, then glanced around the table at his sons. "Why are you guys so upset? Usually you're thrilled to ditch a baby-sitter."

"We liked her," Jack, Jr., mumbled without looking at his dad.

"Yeah, she made us cookies and milk for snacks, and she read us stories at bedtime before she tucked us in. She even made Jack, Jr., a Ninja Turtle cake to take to his Cub Scout meeting." David swiped a hand beneath his nose, a sure sign that tears weren't far away. "And I think she likes us, too."

"I'm sure she does like you guys. What's not to like?" Jack leaned over and ruffled David's hair. "But she isn't your baby-sitter. I hired her to teach you fellows some manners, and she was kind enough to help out for a while until I could find a new housekeeper."

Jack, Jr., snapped up his head, alarm written all over his face. "You hired a new housekeeper?"

Jack frowned while he toyed with one of the two forks on the place mat, wondering if his sons knew which one to use for what purpose. He sure as hell didn't. "Not exactly. But I put an ad in the paper."

"Why don't you hire Malinda?" Jack, Jr., suggested, his voice rising in excitement. "I bet she'd say yes."

"Oh, I don't know, son..."

Darren climbed onto Jack's lap. "I bet she would, Dad." He wrapped an arm around Jack's shoulder and looked up at him, his eyes wide and pleading. "'Specially if you asked real nice."

The mail scattered beneath the front door's slot nearly covered the entry hall floor. Malinda grimaced as she stooped to scrape it into a neat pile. Her frown deepened when she noted the return address on several envelopes was the same. Collection Bureau of America. Gracious, how she detested that name.

And it wasn't as if she needed to be reminded on a daily basis that she owed the money, she thought as she scooped the mail from the floor. The debts were hers—or rather Aunt Hattie's—and she was determined to pay them. The only problem was they were so huge! Working three jobs wasn't even enough.

"Make that two jobs," she mumbled despondently, remembering her hasty retreat from the Brannans' home. She hadn't even waited around long enough to receive the money due her. And judging by Jack's mood when she'd last seen him, she might never get it.

Tears brimmed in her eyes and Malinda flopped down on the floor, cradling the mail on her lap. There were days— today in particular—when she was tempted to take her parents' offer of money, pay off the debts and get on with her life.

Drawing in a shaky breath, she dropped her head back against the wall and stared at the ceiling. Aunt Hattie's ceiling. Aunt Hattie's house. Malinda knew she could sell the house and use the profits to pay off the debts. Aunt Hattie had encouraged her to do just that before she'd died.

Tears filled her eyes again, blurring the hairline cracks in the ceiling's plaster. But she couldn't bring herself to sell. This was Aunt Hattie's house. The house where her aunt had been born and had lived her entire life. The home she'd willingly shared with Malinda. No. Malinda couldn't sell it. Not yet anyway.

Jack stood on Malinda's doorstep calling himself three kinds of a fool. Why he'd let the boys talk him into this was beyond him. Malinda had already refused his offer of employment once—no, make that twice.

He glanced in the direction of the driveway where his Blazer was parked and rolled his eyes. All four boys were lined up at the passenger window, their noses pressed against the glass.

There was no escaping this confrontation. Not if his sons had any say in the matter.

He lifted a fist to the front door and knocked. Almost immediately the door opened. Malinda stood opposite, her nose red, her eyes watery. Jack felt a lead weight hit the bottom of his stomach and recognized it for what it was. Guilt. The boys were right. He had made her cry.

She sniffed and hugged her arms beneath her breasts. "Yes?"

The ice in her voice was as cold and debilitating as the wind cutting through his jacket. She wasn't going to make this apology easy on him, he could see that. But who could blame her? "Mind if I come in? It's kind of cold out."

Malinda would rather have slammed the door in his face, but her upbringing made her offer politely, "I'm sorry. Please come in." She stepped back, making room for him to pass.

Once inside, Jack paused, glancing around. The house was old. Sturdy, but in definite need of repair. And cold. Almost as cold as the temperature outside. He shivered and stuck his hands into his pockets, seeking warmth.

The telltale movement didn't escape Malinda's eyes. "I'm sorry it's so chilly in here," she said in apology. "Since I was gone for the week, I turned the furnace off." She could have added that she'd turned it off to save money, but she didn't. She had her pride. Instead she gestured toward the back hallway. "Why don't we go into the kitchen? It's warmer there and I was just about to make a pot of coffee."

Jack followed her down the dimly lit hall. While she filled the percolator with water, he took a seat at the oak breakfast table. A white linen cloth, embroidered with intricate trails of ivy and flowers, covered the table. Jack molded his hands to his thighs, careful not to touch the pristine cloth. As uncomfortable with the silence as he was with the white cloth, he cleared his throat and said, "Nice house."

Malinda turned to look at him to see if he'd made the comment in jest. Although her home was filled with family heirlooms and neat to the point of obsession, she knew the house itself was old, outdated and falling apart at the seams. In comparison, Jack lived in a palace.

His innocent expression convinced her he was sincere. "Thank you," she said before returning to her task of measuring coffee grounds.

"Is it yours or do you rent?"

Malinda dumped the grounds into the brewing basket and blew out a frustrated breath. Polite conversation. People did it all the time, but she wasn't in the mood for polite conversation. Jack Brannan had a purpose for this visit and it appeared it was up to her to force the issue. She jammed the percolator's cord into the wall socket, then took the seat opposite him. She smiled politely, hoping to sweeten the bite in her next statement. "It's mine. Aunt Hattie left it to me. But I'm sure you didn't come here to discover whether or not I own my home. Just exactly why are you here?"

The bluntness of her question caught Jack totally off guard. The only answer he could come up with was the truth. "The kids made me do it." At her surprised look, he laughed. "They were upset when you left and mad at me because I'd made you cry." He stretched a hand across the table and caught hers in his. "I'm sorry I yelled at you."

He was a toucher. Malinda had seen evidence enough of that in the short time she'd known him, yet the gesture was almost her undoing. The warmth and tenderness in his grasp took her breath, but it was the look of remorse she found in his eyes that touched her heart. Unable to meet the intensity of his gaze, she dipped her head to stare at their hands. "An apology isn't necessary," she said softly.

He chuckled, remembering his sons' insistence on that very issue. "Oh, yes. Definitely necessary." Lacing his fingers through hers, he, too, stared at their joined hands, his mood once again thoughtful. "And maybe an explanation, too."

He frowned, leaning back in his chair and drawing her hand to his side of the table. "When I pulled that shirt out of my closet, it brought back a whole lot of bad memories." He rubbed the ball of his thumb across her manicured nails. "Laurel used to starch my shirts. Or rather she sent them out to be starched. To her that was a sign we'd arrived. She'd married a carpenter, but when my business took off she expected me to turn into some kind of hotshot business executive. Someone she could drag to the country club and all the social events and show off. She thought by putting me in a starched shirt and filling my closet with three-piece suits, she could make me into that someone." He shook his head sadly. "It didn't work. I couldn't be the man she wanted me to be."

His chest rose and fell on a weary sigh. "From the time the twins were born, our marriage went from heaven to hell. She left me twice, the last time when Patrick was two months old. She died in a car wreck with a man I didn't even know."

He glanced up from their joined hands, drawing Malinda's gaze, as well. The pain in his eyes pulled at her. "I know it wasn't fair of me to take out my frustrations on you, but finding starched shirts in my closet was a reminder of a bad time in my life, a time I'd rather forget."

Not knowing what to say, Malinda squeezed her fingers around his broad palm.

He offered her a halfhearted smile. "But the apology is only half the reason I'm here." He puffed his cheeks and blew out a slow breath, knowing the worst part of this confrontation was yet to come. "You see, the boys really fell for you and they—I mean, we—wondered if you might consider coming back and living with us again." He felt her fingers tense in his. "Just give us a chance," he added quickly before she could say no.

Malinda shook her head. "It just wouldn't work. I—"

At that precise moment a drip of water splattered against their joined hands. Another hit the cloth to the right. In slow motion, both Malinda and Jack lifted their chins, looking toward the ceiling. Water marked the plaster in a large, dark circle that already sagged with the added weight.

"Oh, no!" Jerking her hand free of his, Malinda ran for the staircase in the front entry with Jack one step behind her. At the top of the stairs, she slid to a stop, clapping her hands over her mouth.

Water pooled on the hallway's hardwood floor and ran in narrow rivulets down its length, constantly fed by the stream seeping from beneath the bathroom door.

Jack quickly assessed the situation. No heat in the house. Temperatures ranging from below zero to freezing for the past week. Inadequate insulation. It didn't take a genius to figure out her water pipes had frozen and burst and left one hell of a mess. Already the hardwood floor was beginning to buckle.

And Malinda wasn't moving. She stood there in front of him, frozen in place, her hands still pressed over her mouth. Immediately he took charge.

"Where's the water main?" he asked. When she didn't answer, he grabbed her by the shoulders and shook. "Malinda! Where's the turnoff for the water main?"

She lifted her face to his, her eyes filled with tears. "The basement," she said in a barely audible whisper. "It's in the basement," she repeated before she turned to stare at the water again.

Her look of despair tore at Jack's heart. He didn't need a palm reader to tell him the cause of the defeated look. Money trouble. And it appeared this particular woman had more than her share.

He caught her elbow and aimed her toward the stairs, successfully obliterating her view of the destruction. "You get the boys out of the car and park them in front of the television," he ordered gently, "while I shut off the main."

* * *

A mutually beneficial agreement, Malinda told herself as she shook out a dress and hung it in the closet. Her house would receive the necessary repairs, she would have a place to stay until the repairs were completed and all with no money expended.

Crossing back to the suitcase, she selected a pile of lingerie and moved to the dresser. In return, she reasoned further, Jack would have a live-in housekeeper and babysitter until the repairs were made. A fair business deal to anyone's mind.

She stacked the lingerie neatly in the drawer and pushed it closed, then looked at her reflection in the dresser's mirror.

"Then why do I feel I've been duped?" she asked hopelessly.

Because, as usual, Jack had stacked the deck in his favor. He'd worked like a Trojan, moving furniture, rolling up rugs, mopping water. Who could say no to a man like that?

And if that hadn't been enough, he'd waited until they were all sitting at her kitchen table sipping hot chocolate, with Patrick firmly ensconced in her lap, before dropping the bomb. Who could say no to his suggestion when four sets of pitiful little eyes were watching you, begging you to say yes?

Sighing, she closed the suitcase lid with a snap. Yes, she'd been outmaneuvered again.

"Need anything?"

Malinda turned to find Jack standing at the bedroom door. There was simply no escaping the man. Stifling a groan, she said, "No, not a thing," and lifted the case from the bed. But before she could move, he was there taking it from her hands. The room suddenly shrank in size.

"Do you have to work Saturday?" he asked as he levered the suitcase to the closet's top shelf. The upward stretch pulled his sweatshirt above his waist, baring a narrow strip of skin.

Malinda swallowed hard and threaded her fingers at her waist and began to twist. "No. Cecile and I alternate Saturdays."

"Good. That'll give us a chance to get started on your house." He dusted off his hands as he turned to face her. One look at her and he heaved a frustrated sigh. He caught her by the elbow and guided her to the bed. "I'm not going to bite you, Malinda."

"I know that," she replied as she nervously smoothed her skirt over her knees.

He hunkered down in front of her and captured her hands in his, sweeping them out, then in, making her arms like bellows. "Then loosen up a little."

"I am loose," she lied.

Jack chuckled and shook his head. "Yeah, and I'm the Pied Piper." Slowly he pushed to his feet, then crossed to the door. Turning back, he offered softly, "Don't worry, Malinda. Everything'll work out great. You'll see."

His optimism did nothing to soothe the churning sensation his touch had stirred in Malinda's stomach.

"—a mutually beneficial agreement."

The words had become a litany. One Malinda had repeated to herself a hundred times over the past week. At the moment, the words were being recited to Cecile as the two worked side by side, steaming wrinkles out of a new shipment of spring dresses.

"Beneficial for whom?" Cecile asked as she pulled another dress from the box.

"Jack." When she saw Cecile's eyebrows shoot up, Malinda added hurriedly, "And me." Ignoring her friend's

dubious look, she took the dress from Cecile and settled i
over the steamer form. "My house receives the necessar
repairs, I have a place to stay while the work is bein
done—all with no money expended—and Jack has a live-ir
baby-sitter and housekeeper until the repairs are finished
A mutually beneficial agreement."

"So you said," Cecile said, biting back a smile.

"Well, it is," Malinda replied defensively.

"Is there a time limit on this 'mutually beneficial agree
ment'?"

The question drew a frown. Malinda pressed her foo
down on the steamer's activator, making the dress's hem
billow out. "Well, no," she replied reluctantly.

"And who will be making these repairs?"

"Jack."

Cecile shook her head as she pulled another dress from
the box. "Malinda, you are a sweet, if naive, fool. The
man's got you right where he wants you. His kids are taken
care of, his house is cleaned and his meals are cooked for
as long as he wants."

"Not for as long as he wants, only until the repairs are
completed."

"You must have forgotten Mr. Adderly."

No, Malinda hadn't forgotten Adderly. He was the man
who had repaired the furnace at Aunt Hattie's house last
winter. "What does he have to do with this?"

Cecile shrugged and handed Malinda the dress. "Nothing. At least not directly. But do you remember how long
it took him to fix the furnace?"

Chills chased down Malinda's back.

"Three months," Cecile stated without waiting for an
answer. "First he had to order the part. That took weeks.
Then the part didn't fit and he had to reorder. When he finally put the part in and the furnace still didn't work, he
discovered something else was broken and he repeated the

whole process." She gave Malinda a knowing look. "The guy got paid by the hour. Meanwhile, you spent the winter running around the house in four layers of clothing. Get the picture?"

Malinda shook off her growing doubts. "Jack isn't Mr. Adderly."

"No, and he isn't Jimmy Johnson, either."

Heat flushed Malinda's cheeks at the mere mention of Jimmy's name. She jerked the freshly steamed dress from the form and thrust it at Cecile to place on a hanger. "No, he isn't Jimmy," she said irritably.

"And he doesn't deserve your defense any more than Jimmy Johnson deserved you defending him."

Malinda snatched another wrinkled dress from the box. "Jimmy Johnson was a nice boy. People just didn't understand him, that's all."

"Oh, they understood him all right. He was a twelve-year-old hoodlum. They just didn't have a crush on him like you did."

Malinda heaved a frustrated breath. They'd had this argument before. The first time at the age of twelve, and on numerous other occasions over the years. She wasn't anxious to repeat it now. "What *is* your point, Cecile?"

"Do you have a crush on Jack Brannan?"

Malinda's fingers dug into the dress's delicate fabric. She forced her fingers to relax and shook the dress out over the form. "Crush is a childish emotion."

"Okay, then. Are you in love with Jack Brannan?"

Malinda's foot hit the activator with a thud and stayed there. Steam hissed at her, misting her face. *In love with Jack Brannan?* Her mind recoiled at the very thought. He was a crude, unbearably domineering man who had the fashion sense of a sixteen-year-old rebel. "I hardly know the man."

"Love knows no sense of time."

"Oh, for pity's sake, Cecile," Malinda said impatiently. "Has he kissed you?"

Malinda grabbed the steamer's water bottle. "We need more water. I'll be right back."

Cecile caught her arm before she could escape. "He has, hasn't he?"

Evasion hadn't daunted her partner, so Malinda tried indifference. "So what if he has?"

Cecile squealed. "Oooh, I just knew it!" She dragged Malinda to the bench against the wall. "Tell me, was it good? I just know it was."

Good? A mild understatement in Malinda's opinion, but then her experience with men was rather limited. She desperately wanted to tell Cecile everything. The kiss. His touch. How it made her insides turn to mush. How she could barely draw a breath in the man's very presence. She needed to talk to someone. Someone with experience who could help her understand the feelings Jack evoked in her.

She just wasn't sure Cecile was that someone.

Oh, her friend had the experience all right. A young widow, Cecile had a constant stream of men in and out of her life.

But she also had a tendency—when given the opportunity—to run Malinda's life.

Malinda cast a furtive glance to the play area where Patrick sat, alternately stacking blocks, then knocking them down with a quiet intensity. So much like his father. Her hands formed a knot in her lap as tight as the one that twisted in her stomach. The same color hair, the same strong chin, the same thin lips. She swallowed hard, forcing back the image of the adult version of those features. "Yes, he kissed me," she blurted out, then added more slowly, "And, yes, it was absolutely wonderful."

Cecile could respect a person's privacy when it suited her. At the moment, it didn't. "So you like the way he kisses,"

he mused. "And you're having a hard time accepting that
act."

Malinda's face throbbed in embarrassment. "Yes," she
vhispered and stole another glance at Patrick. "What am
going to do?"

"You're going to let him kiss you again." Malinda surged
o her feet, but Cecile hauled her back, forcing her to re-
nain at her side. "And you're not going to feel guilty about
t, either," she warned. "You've lived by Aunt Hattie's
ules long enough."

Smug in her role as adviser, Cecile settled her spine more
comfortably against the wall. "First we have to teach you
now to relax." She was silent a moment, thoughtfully
vorking her lower lip between her teeth. "Belly breaths,"
he finally advised. "At least two, then—"

"Belly breaths!" Malinda repeated in horror. "What in
he world are belly breaths?"

"Deep breaths. Don't use your diaphragm." She pressed
Malinda's hand against her own abdomen and demon-
strated. "Now you try it."

Malinda blew out a disbelieving breath, but at Cecile's
hreatening glare she dutifully attempted a "belly
oreath"—and felt like a fool.

"Great! Now don't you feel more relaxed?"

Malinda narrowed an eye at her. "No, I feel like an idiot." Shaking her head, she stood. "Although I appreciate
your help, Cecile, this just isn't going to work. I'm not like
you. I just can't relax around a man."

"Sure you can," Cecile said, rising to stand by Malinda.
"You just need a little practice, that's all. Now this is what
you should do..."

Seven

"You're sure Jason can handle the boys?" Malinda asked anxiously as she snapped her seat belt in place.

"Positive. He's seventeen, responsible and the kids idolize him."

"But what if there's an emergency?"

"I left your number by the phone. He'll call if he runs up against something he can't handle." Jack turned the key in the ignition, then stretched an arm across the width of the Blazer and squeezed Malinda's neck in reassurance. "Relax. The boys'll be fine."

Relax? Malinda had heard that particular word often enough over the past week to last her a lifetime. And Cecile was wrong. Practice was *not* what she needed. A frontal lobotomy, maybe, but not practice. Malinda knew this because her abdominal muscles ached from the number of belly breaths she had tried. And they hadn't helped one iota. She still froze up every time Jack got within a foot of

ᴇr. And today she was expected to spend the entire day
ᴡith him—alone!

She'd used every excuse she could come up with to avoid
his particular form of torture. She had pointed out that she
ᴋnew absolutely nothing about plumbing repair, to which
ɦe'd responded, "I don't need your knowledge. Just an-
ᴏther set of hands." Malinda glanced at her gloved hands
ᴀnd frowned. She couldn't very well deny she'd been born
ᴍinus that set of appendages.

Then she had mentioned she had a lot of housework to
ᴅo: laundry, vacuuming and dusting. He'd assured her that
ɦe'd help her complete her tasks that night. "After all,"
ɦe'd said, "two people can accomplish a job twice as fast
as one." Malinda nearly groaned, remembering.

Her last hope had been the boys. If they went along,
ᴛhey'd get in Jack's way while he worked, she'd reasoned.
And if they remained at home, who would watch over
ᴛhem? At almost that precise moment the doorbell had rung
ᴀnd Jason appeared. So much for the boys' welfare as an
excuse to remain at home, which left Malinda free to serve
as Jack's extra set of hands for the day.

As he wheeled the Blazer onto her drive, Malinda forced
herself to think positively. By helping Jack, the repair work
ᴏn the house would be accomplished quicker and she would
be present, seeing that the work was completed in a timely
manner, thus putting to rest the doubts Cecile had raised
when she'd mentioned Mr. Adderly's name.

For some reason she didn't find these positive thoughts
particularly comforting.

She didn't find them any more comforting when she repeated them to herself two hours later as she stood penned
against the bathroom wall by Jack's shoulder, holding a
wrench around a section of pipe while he wielded a blowtorch below.

His shoulder was lodged against her abdomen, his bent knee against her shin. She couldn't have budged an inch even if she'd dared.

The man was a slave driver. They hadn't rested a second since they'd entered the house. Furniture had been moved and stacked, carpets rolled up and stashed in the garage. A hole big enough to walk through had been knocked in the bathroom wall. Malinda glanced down at Jack and silently prayed he knew what he was doing.

"Almost done. Hold what you've got," he instructed as he swiped his forearm across his forehead before aiming the torch at a new section of pipe.

Heat diffused Malinda's face—from the blowtorch or the proximity to Jack, she couldn't be sure. She couldn't take her eyes off the man. He'd shoved his sweatshirt to his elbows and now a fine mist of perspiration gleamed on his bare arms. Mesmerized by the play of fire reflected in the beads of perspiration, Malinda stared. Muscles rippled and veins stood out beneath his tanned skin. She traced a vein with her gaze, from his elbow to his wrist, and yearned to trace it with a fingertip. His hands were strong, yet she knew his touch to be gentle. She'd felt that gentleness once at her cheek, just before he'd kissed her that day in the snow. Again when he'd dared her to touch him that night in his study. But touching him, she'd discovered, was like sticking a finger into an electrical outlet.

Absorbed and totally distracted from her responsibilities as helper by her wandering thoughts, she loosened her grip on the wrench. The tool slipped, and before she could right it, the blowtorch cut through the section of pipe Jack was working on. Without the wrench to hold it in place, the pipe broke loose. It slammed against Jack's shoulder, knocking the torch from his hands and his butt to the floor.

Without thinking, Malinda grabbed for the pipe.

"Don't touch that! It's—"

His warning came too late. Malinda screamed and dropped the pipe like the hot potato it was. Jack ducked to avoid a second encounter with the hot metal and rolled to his feet. He had Malinda's hands in his before the first tear rolled down her cheek.

His fingers formed a bracelet around her wrists as he turned her hands up. Her pulse throbbed beneath his thumb. Angry red stripes streaked both palms. A muscle twitched in his jaw as he lifted his gaze to hers.

"I'm okay," she said in a quivery voice and tried to pull away. "It just scared me, that's all."

But Jack wouldn't let go. "We need to put something on this." He nodded his head toward the medicine cabinet. "Anything in there for burns?"

Unable to speak, Malinda merely nodded.

Still holding her wrists, he guided her to the tub and settled her on its edge. After rummaging through the cabinet, he returned carrying a tube of ointment and a roll of gauze. He knelt and took her hands in his, turning them palms up. He bent his head, touching his lips to first one palm, then the other.

Fresh tears sprang to Malinda's eyes.

"I always kiss the boys' boo-boos," he said softly. "Makes them heal faster." He took the tube of ointment and squeezed a blob onto the tip of his finger and began smearing it across the angry red stripe. His touch was soft, gentle. A feather moving across her palm. Yet heat raced up her arm and throughout her body, twisting her stomach into knots and sending shivers chasing down her spine.

"Did I hurt you?" he asked in concern when he felt the tremble.

"No," she lied. "Just a reaction, I guess."

He continued to talk to her, his voice as soothing as the stroke of his fingers, but Malinda hadn't a clue what he was saying. Heat glazed her eyes and dulled her ability to think.

He took the gauze and wound it around her hand—winding her nerves even tighter—then picked up the opposite hand and began the process all over again. Malinda thought she'd die if he didn't finish quickly.

Belly breaths, she reminded herself. Two belly breaths, Cecile had promised, and this tension would fade away. She closed her eyes and sucked in the first one, held it to the count of ten, then slowly released it.

She waited a minute, measuring. Nothing. Her stomach still churned and her eyes burned behind closed lids. *It takes two,* she told herself and drew in the second. She'd reached the count of six when she felt hands cinch her waist and a firm tug. She opened her eyes, but before she had a chance to catch herself she was sprawled in Jack's lap.

"What are you doing?" she said, gasping.

"You looked like you were about to pass out. Thought I'd save you the fall."

Malinda struggled to sit up. "I wasn't going to faint, I was doing deep-breathing exercises."

Jack allowed her room enough to straighten but not to rise. "For the pain?"

"No, not for the pain," Malinda replied impatiently, giving the hem of her sweater a tug. "To relax."

"Are you tense?" he asked, a grin chipping at one corner of his mouth.

Malinda nearly screamed in frustration. "Yes, I'm tense! For some stupid reason, every time I get near you my stomach twists up in knots."

He laid a palm against her cheek and forced her to look at him. "Why?"

The question was one-word simple, the look in his eyes was not. Understanding, compassion and, yes, even desire, turned his brown eyes soft.

Malinda swallowed hard. "I don't know," she lied, averting her gaze to the gaping hole in the wall. "It just happens."

Jack caught her cheek again, turning her face to his. "I think I know why."

Malinda's eyes grew wide in alarm. "You do?"

"Mmm-hmm." He settled her more comfortably in his lap. "When people tense up it's a sure sign they're fighting something." He pulled at his chin and eyed Malinda thoughtfully. "I think you're attracted to me and it scares the hell out of you."

The truth in his statement had Malinda squirming to free herself from the trap he'd created with his legs. "This is ridiculous. Please let me go."

Jack just smiled. "It's not ridiculous. In fact, I'm attracted to you, too."

That announcement stilled Malinda's struggles. She glanced up at him, her mouth slightly agape. "You are?" she asked incredulously.

"Yep. And that scares the hell out of me, too." He brushed a straggle of hair from her forehead. "But it sure as hell doesn't make me want to run. It makes me want to test."

"Test?" she repeated, her voice a husky whisper.

"Yeah, you know, see if the real thing is as pleasurable as what I've imagined."

Malinda's cheek flamed in embarrassment. She knew without a doubt whatever test he administered would be pleasurable. She hadn't forgotten that first kiss in the snow. But he was experienced in these things and she wasn't.

There was no way she could pass *his* test. "And if it's not?" she asked uncertainly.

"Then we'll both have our answer, won't we?"

Malinda chewed at her lower lip a moment, weighing the consequences. "What will this test consist of?"

"Well..." He frowned a minute, thinking. "Tension comes from suppression, so what we'll do is quit suppressing. For example—" He lifted his hands to her hair and pulled out a pin. "You always wear your hair up, but I can't forget that first night you spent with us, when it was down."

First one pin, then another, hit the floor. "With it up, you look like some dried-up old maid." She raised a defensive hand to her bun at the unfavorable description, but he batted it away. He shook her hair free and buried his fingers in it, running them through its length, then cupped his palms beneath her chin and tipped her face up to his. A smile that would melt ice crooked one corner of his mouth. "But with it down you look like one hell of a woman." He touched his lips to hers, nibbled lightly, then withdrew. "Now it's your turn. What are you suppressing?" he asked softly.

Her eyelids were so heavy Malinda could barely hold them up. "Do that again," she whispered weakly.

"What?"

"Kiss me."

Jack chuckled and lowered his mouth over hers. He knew her innocence, her inexperience. He'd seen it in her eyes, tasted it on her lips, felt it in the tentative climb of her fingertips up his chest. It only endeared her to him that much more. He traced the fullness of her lower lip, then moved to sketch her upper lip's near-perfect bow.

Her mouth parted beneath his on a low moan. The sound chipped away at a self-control he wasn't aware he pos-

sessed. He wrapped his arms around her, drawing her
nearer, settling her more snugly against his groin.

"Kiss me back, Lindy," he murmured against her lips.

Her eyes flipped open wide and full of fear. "I can't."

He kissed first one eyelid, then the other, closed again.
"Yes, you can. Don't suppress. Let yourself go."

When she didn't move, he feared she was more emotionally handicapped than he'd first suspected. Then a
tentative hand climbed from his chest to his cheek and
rested there. He felt the thunder of her pulse and knew how
much even that small a gesture had cost her. The knowledge humbled him. Tucking her head beneath his chin, he
lay back, ignoring the water and rubble that cut into his
spine as he stretched out on the floor, and settled her
against his length.

For a moment they just lay there, unmoving. A lifetime
of restraint kept Malinda's hands still. But Jack knew no
such restraint. His fingers moved in small, hypnotic circles
at her waist, inching her sweater higher and higher on her
back. Cool air hit her bare skin and a shiver chased down
her spine.

At her bra strap, his fingers stopped, fumbled a moment, then moved steadily upward, kneading away at tight
muscles. Tension melted from her body at his touch, leaving her limp and vulnerable. She raised her head and met
his gaze . . . and saw the devil in his eyes and in his smile.

She'd known this man was dangerous. She knew, with
him, she didn't stand a chance. Knowing that, she lowered
her mouth to his and allowed her lips the freedom to roam
and explore.

Textures and tastes abounded. Lips that to the eye had
seemed thin and uncompromising, parted beneath hers to
reveal a softness and fullness that both surprised and teased
her. A whiskered chin sanded hers. Noses bumped and

faces sought new angles. Tongues touched, mated and darted away to explore once again.

Up until this moment Malinda would never have dared to give in to such sensual pleasures. Aunt Hattie had trained her well. The men in her life had been few—safe, undemanding male versions of herself. Dates had consisted of quiet dinners, an evening at the symphony or perhaps a stimulating lecture at the university, and all had ended with a chaste kiss at her door.

Nothing like this, she thought wildly as Jack's hands roamed her back. His palms molded to her sides, then slipped around to cup her bared breasts. Nothing *ever* like this, she thought on a ragged sigh.

His thumb flicked over first one nipple, then the other. They peaked and bloomed beneath his touch. Desire ripped through Malinda like a knife.

It is a man's nature to let his passions rule. But a woman must rule her passions.

A bucket of ice water dumped on her back would have had less impact than Aunt Hattie's untimely advice. Malinda was on her feet and grabbing at her clothes in the blink of an eye.

Jack struggled to his feet. "Is something wrong?" he asked in concern.

Straining to clasp her bra, Malinda avoided his gaze. "No. I'm sorry, I—"

Jack brushed her hands away, turned her around and gathered her bra straps in his hands. "Sorry for what?"

Malinda's breath lodged in her throat when his fingers brushed her back. "I'm sorry I permitted things to go so far," she managed to say as he slipped the hook into place. "A lady should never allow a man such liberties."

Her sweater came down with a hard jerk. Jack caught her by the elbow and whirled her around. His eyes met hers and held. "Well, I'm not sorry," he stated flatly. "But if I were going to be sorry for anything, I'd be sorry we didn't finish what we started."

Pricing manuals were fanned out across the desk. Lumber, plumbing, paint, electrical. Neat columns of numbers were aligned beside each item listed. A blueprint of the proposed building lay beneath the books, the architects specifications spelled out in the corner of each page. Jack had spent hours studying the plans, accumulating information and needed materials. Now it was only a matter of figuring the footage, the costs and extending the prices.

But Jack couldn't add two plus two and come up with four. His ability to concentrate was shot to hell, his mind on everything but work.

Not everything, he amended mentally as he tapped his pencil against the edge of his desk in frustration. *Just Malinda.* The woman was slowly driving him crazy. She sashayed through his house every morning, cooking breakfast, making beds and coaxing the boys into their clothes. Their lunch boxes in hand, she stood at the front door inspecting for hats and mittens and zipped-up coats. With a special message for each—a good luck to Jack, Jr., on his math test, a reminder to David to give his teacher the apple she'd added to his lunch, and to Darren a gentle warning to drink all his milk—she'd whisk them out the door to meet their bus. Then she'd gather up Patrick and a mountainous bag of paraphernalia and they'd zip out the door for work.

And she did all this dressed as if she were attending a tea party. Where'd she find the time? No matter what time he got up, she was up ahead of him, dressed and ready for the day. They'd agreed Sunday would be her day off, but she'd spent the first one cleaning out the boys' closets and dresser drawers. The second ironing patches on jeans and building a castle out of Lego plastic building blocks with Patrick on the floor in the den.

After they were all in bed, he could hear her in his study typing away at that ridiculous column she wrote for the paper. She found time for everything...but him. And that was the rub.

He was man enough to admit he was attracted to her...and wise enough to know he shouldn't be. They didn't have a single thing in common. He was a lump of coal to her polished diamond. Where she was neat to the point of obsession, he was—well, he was a slob. He liked sweatshirts and jeans. She liked silk and lace. He liked cold beer and Monday night football. She preferred wine and classical music. Those things alone should have warned him off. They didn't. Instead they intrigued him even more.

And he suspected she was attracted to him, as well. Hell, there were some things a man just knew. But every time he got near her, she tensed up like a coiled spring. Knowing this, he'd purposefully tricked her into going to her house with him to work on the repairs in order to have her alone for a while, away from the boys. He'd hoped that by spending some time with him—a little one-on-one—she'd relax, feeling a little more at ease. And his plan had worked—for a while, anyway.

But just when things had really heated up, when he thought he'd broken through whatever barriers restricted her, she'd frozen up again. *What went wrong?* he wondered as he studied the sharp point on his pencil.

No answer was forthcoming. He really hadn't expected one. Malinda was the only one who could answer that question and he wasn't even sure *she* knew the answer. Because of that, he'd avoided her like the plague since Saturday. Partly out of anger, partly out of frustration. He

rowned at the papers and manuals cluttering his desk. And
partly because he had more work than he could say grace
over.

Ain't love hell?

The pencil snapped between Jack's fingers, the two jag-
ged pieces hitting the floor and rolling beneath his desk.
Where had *that* come from, he wondered as he dragged a
shaky hand through his hair. In an attempt to escape the
abominable question, he pushed to his feet and paced the
length of his office.

It didn't work. The word *love* chased him, bunching up
the muscles in his neck and making his head throb with a
dull ache.

Groaning, he crossed back to his desk and dropped
weakly into his chair. It was all her fault. She'd pranced into
their lives, cleaning and organizing and anticipating their
every need. It was only natural he'd grow to depend on her.
And depending on someone was not necessarily love, he
assured himself.

He waited for the relief to come, for the dull ache in his
head to disappear. It didn't.

He rolled his wrist to glance at his watch. Nine o'clock.
And he wasn't any closer to finishing the bid than when
he'd started at six.

Shoving the thoughts of Malinda from his mind, he
cleared the total from the calculator and began once again
to feed in numbers.

Malinda sat at the kitchen table, compiling a grocery list.
Behind her, the dishwasher hummed its way through the
heat cycle accompanied by the rhythmic thump of towels
tumbling in the clothes dryer in the laundry room. They
were the only sounds in the house. The boys were long since
tucked in for the night.

Remembering they were out of laundry detergent, Malinda added it to her list, then scribbled "industrial strength" in the margin. Toilet tissue, laundry detergent, peanut butter and jelly, Cheerios cereal for Patrick, Fruit Loops cereal for Jack, Jr., Frosted Flakes cereal for the twins, chips for school lunches, shaving cream and razor blades for Jack. Malinda couldn't help smiling as she reviewed the list. It was so different from those she'd compiled for herself in the past.

Variety. That was the difference. Her grocery shopping had been boring and dull in comparison. Not so with the Brannans'. Every male in the house had his own likes and dislikes. What one enjoyed, the other despised. It was a challenge trying to please them all.

And you love every minute of it, she admitted, yawning sleepily. She glanced at the clock on the oven door. The yawn quickly dissolved into a frown. Jack was late again. He'd promised to be home by seven so he could have dinner with the boys and help Jack, Jr., with his science project. Yet dinner had been served hours ago and a working volcano sat on the table at her left. All conducted without the presence or assistance of Jack Brannan.

Malinda wrinkled her nose at the hulking mass of papier-mâché. Chicken wire, torn newspaper, a ton of watered-down glue and three bottles of paint. Artistically, she admitted, the project was a success. Scientifically she feared it failed miserably. Science had never been her forte.

Jack, Jr., had needed his father's help, which was why Malinda was still up. She intended to have a serious talk with him concerning his duties as a father. For a week, ever since they'd worked on the plumbing at her house, he had avoided her—and as a result his sons. Their conversations were short and terse. Their meetings fleeting moments as hey passed in the hall either on their way to work or on their way to bed.

And Malinda regretted that. She also regretted having said she was sorry she had let things go too far. For that short space of time on the bathroom floor, she'd felt more alive than she ever had in her entire life. Every nerve ending in her body had pulsed with a need she could neither name nor understand . . . but she wanted to. Gracious, how she wanted to feel that way again.

But it appeared if left up to Jack, she wouldn't. He'd carefully avoided being alone with her ever since. And she regretted that.

A beam of headlights cut an arc across the opposite wall. Malinda rose to her feet. He was home.

A key turned in the back door and immediately she tensed. "Two belly breaths," she whispered, her hands already twisting at her waist. She barely had time to draw in the first one before Jack stepped through the door.

Breathe, Malinda, she screamed inwardly. *Remember to breathe!*

"Hi." Without looking at her, Jack shrugged out of his coat and draped it over a kitchen chair. "The boys in bed?"

Caught in the middle of a belly breath, Malinda's "yes" came out on a strangled whoosh of air.

Jack didn't seem to notice, his attention was centered on the volcano. Groaning, he slapped the heel of his hand against his forehead. "Damn. I forgot all about the science project." He crossed to the table and peered down the volcano's mouth. "Good job." He glanced at Malinda. "Did you help him?"

"Yes, but he did most of the work. Structurally it's sound, but we couldn't figure out how to make the silly thing erupt."

"Baking soda and vinegar." Jack dragged out a chair and sat down, already adjusting the container Malinda had concealed within the volcano's cone.

"It's a shame you weren't here a few hours ago. We could have used your expertise."

His head bent over the volcano, he mumbled, "Had a bid I had to get out." He stretched out a hand without looking at her. "Hand me some baking soda."

Malinda dutifully placed the box in his hand, then went to the pantry for the vinegar. "He was disappointed, you know."

Their hands brushed as he took the vinegar bottle from her. Lightning struck and abated at the contact. He glanced up, then back down at the volcano's mouth. "He'll get over it."

"Maybe."

He looked up again, one eyebrow arched in a neat V. "Maybe?"

Malinda shrugged and sat down next to him. "Children are resilient. They get over things, but they don't necessarily forget."

"I'll make it up to him," he said, returning his attention to the volcano.

"I'm sure you will," she agreed, "but was the bid more important than helping your son with his project?"

"It's not a matter of importance. It's a matter of priorities. Work comes first."

"Why?"

Jack rolled his eyes as he leveled a heaping spoonful of baking soda into the narrow cone. "I'd think the answer would be obvious."

"To you, maybe."

He heaved a frustrated breath and dropped both the box and the spoon to the table. "Look, Malinda. I know Jack, r., was disappointed because I wasn't here to help him with his project and I'm sorry about that. But the fact remains that I have to work. I have to prepare bids and get them in on time in order to win construction contracts because *that* is what puts bread on the table."

"You do a lot more than put bread on the table. You give your sons their every heart's desire. There isn't a toy or gadget they don't own and there isn't a sport or an activity they miss out on."

"And what's wrong with that?"

"Nothing, if their other needs are met, as well."

"And you're an expert on the needs of children," he said dryly.

"No, not an expert, but I know what my life was like as a child. My parents provided me with everything money could buy when the only thing I ever wanted was them."

Her statement drew a puzzled frown. "I thought your Aunt Hattie raised you."

"She did, from the age of eight on. My father's business took him overseas and my mother went with him. They left me with a series of nannies and housekeepers and came home for token visits every couple of months. I rebelled. In desperation they parked me with Aunt Hattie."

Jack's hand circled the vinegar bottle and he tilted it, watching the golden liquid roll from side to side. His upbringing hadn't been that different from Malinda's. His parents hadn't wanted him, either. But they'd never sent money. And they'd never made token visits. He righted the bottle and cocked his head to look at her. "We're quite a pair. Two orphans nobody ever really wanted. But there's one important difference. Money. Your parents provided for you. Mine spent whatever they had on booze."

He laid the bottle on its side and spun it around. "Do you know what it's like to grow up without anything?" He didn't wait for an answer. He didn't need one. He'd lived it. "It's hell. Charities provided my clothes and whatever Christmas presents I got. There was never money for Little League or Boy Scouts or any of the other activities the other kids were involved in. I want my boys to have what I never had. Can you understand that?"

"Yes, I understand, but that is *your* need, not the boys'." She laid her hand on top of his. "Jack, children don't need much, they just need a lot of it."

He didn't dare move. He didn't think she was even aware she'd touched him. She was so intent on pleading the boys' case, she'd forgotten about herself and her silly inhibitions. Careful not to disturb her hand, he asked, "And what do you think they need?"

"You," she said simply, then added, "Your love and your attention."

Jack absorbed that for a minute. Yes, he knew his sons needed him. And he tried hard to meet all their needs, both physical and emotional. But he was only one man. He didn't have a wife to share that burden with. There were times when he was so bone-dead tired, so mentally exhausted from work, he feared he wasn't doing the best job of meeting those needs. But he was trying, damn it. He wondered if Malinda realized how hard.

He cocked his head to look at her. She'd shared with him a glimpse of her childhood. He could still see the pain of those memories reflected in her eyes. As a child, her needs had been simple. A mother, a father, a home. She'd been denied two out of the three. But what were her needs as an adult? After living with her for the past few weeks, he suspected those needs hadn't changed much.

Granted, she might not need a mother and father anymore, but she needed a family, a home. He'd seen her with

the boys. Witnessed the way her eyes lit up when she inter-
acted with them, heard her laughter when she'd play with
Patrick. He sensed more than felt her need for him, as well.

He turned his palm up and laced his fingers through hers.
"And what are your needs, Malinda?" he asked softly.

Her cheeks flamed at the sudden change in conversation
and she tried to withdraw her hand. Jack simply tightened
his grip.

"We were discussing the boys," she reminded him firmly.

"Yes, we were," he agreed.

His thumb moved in slow circles on her palm. Malinda
was finding it more and more difficult to concentrate, but
she had to. For the boys' sake. "For the past week, you've
barely seen them. You leave when they do and come home
after they're in bed. I feel responsible."

"Oh? And why would you be responsible?"

"Because I think you're avoiding me, and by avoiding me
you are avoiding them, as well."

"Is that a fact? And why would I be avoiding you?"

"Be-because of what happened," she stammered.

"And what happened, Malinda?"

She lifted her chin a notch and glared at him. "You know
very well what happened."

A smile pulled at the corner of his mouth as he tugged at
her hand, pulling her from the chair to his lap. He knew
very well what had happened. He wondered if she did.

He stretched an arm around either side of her and picked
up two spoons from the table. The movement caused his
arms to press against the sides of her breasts. Heat flooded
Malinda's body at the unexpected contact.

He dipped the spoons into the baking-soda box, then
drew them out, heaping. He lifted his left hand. "This is a
man," he said, then lifted his right. "And this is a woman."

He dumped both spoonfuls of baking soda into the volcano's mouth, then picked up the bottle of vinegar.

"And this," he said as he unscrewed the lid, "is attraction."

He held the bottle over the volcano's mouth and poured. The liquid hit the dry powder with a startling hiss and immediately bubbles erupted, pouring over the top of the volcano and down its sides. "And this," he said, "is what happens when all the ingredients are present."

Malinda's mouth went dry. She couldn't take her eyes off the bubbling liquid. She felt as if that same effervescence bubbled through her veins, the heat of Jack's thighs beneath her feeding those bubbles to near-boiling point.

He reared back in the chair, settling her more comfortably on his lap. "If you noticed, when the man and woman first connected, nothing happened. *But* when we added in the third ingredient, attraction, a chemical reaction took place. Not unlike that which takes place in the human body."

He took a deep breath. Malinda felt the swell of his chest against her back.

"To answer your original question," he said, releasing the breath on a weary sigh. "I have been avoiding you. And it's because of that chemical reaction. Personally I can handle the attraction. In fact, I wouldn't mind experimenting with it a little more. Unfortunately I don't think you can."

Malinda dipped her head, embarrassed by her inadequacies as a woman. "I'm not sure I can, either," she murmured. Then she surprised him by lifting her head and looking him square in the eye. "But I'd like to try."

Jack didn't trust his ears. He stuck a finger in one and swirled. "What did you say?"

"I said I'd like to try. I'm not saying it'll be easy or comfortable at first. But I would like to try." She smoothed her skirt over her knees, carefully averting her gaze as she added, "That is, if you're willing."

Eight

Willing? A stud horse corralled with a mare in heat couldn't be any more willing. But something told Jack he'd better go slow. Malinda was different from most women. Fragile, innocent, bound up by a set of archaic rules he couldn't even imagine.

She was also starved for love—both to give and receive. He'd seen the way she soaked up all Patrick's hugs and wet kisses. He'd seen evidence of it in her care for the three older boys.

But with him she froze up. And that's what worried him. He wasn't a man long on patience. "Tender" to him was a term used to judge a steak. And Malinda needed both patience and tenderness. He wasn't sure he had it in him to meet those needs.

But when she tilted her face to his, her eyes filled with a lifetime of insecurities and self-doubt, he knew he had to try.

He caught her hand in his and slowly pulled it to his lips. "More than willing," he murmured against the baby-soft skin.

His tongue flicked out and set a fire in the hollow of her palm. The heat quickly spread up her arm and down to her toes. She fought the urge to bolt and run and instead focused on his face. His hair was swept straight back, styled by fingers, no comb. His hairline receded slightly on either side of his forehead, shaping a widow's peak a good three inches above his nose.

Worry lines stretched between his brows. She touched a finger to them and wondered at their cause. Work? Responsibilities? Fatigue? She traced them, knowing it could be either one or all. He worked long hours, too long to her way of thinking. And heaven knew, the boys were a huge responsibility. She hoped her presence in his home had lightened that load somewhat.

She had no way to judge the amount of sleep he received, but often she heard him roaming the house at night. Checking on the boys, raiding the kitchen, knocking around in his study. She smoothed a finger down the deepset lines and experienced a flush of pleasure when they melted beneath her touch.

She sought his gaze. Brown eyes watched her beneath a sweep of lashes without a hint of curl. Not a smidgen of doubt or reluctance did she find in the brown depths, though she searched for both. Without moving her gaze from his, she trailed a finger down the slight crook on his nose to rest on his lips.

His mouth opened beneath her fingertips, startling her. Before she could react, he caught her hand in his as he drew one finger deep into the moist cavern and gently sucked. Shivers chased down her spine as he dragged her finger down the length of his tongue, wrapping it in the most erotic of cocoons. Malinda tried hard to swallow and discovered she couldn't. Slowly, oh so slowly, he pulled her finger through puckered lips.

He crooked a smile as he shifted her on his lap.

Every nerve ending in her body awakened and throbbing, Malinda rocketed to her feet. "I'm s-sorry," she stammered. "I must be killing your legs."

Jack caught her hips and pulled her back down, chuckling. "You're killing something, but not my legs." He twisted her around until she sat sideways across his thighs. The action did nothing to relieve the pressure in his jeans. "How 'bout the couch?" he asked and tucked an arm beneath her knees.

She couldn't decide which to grab first when he picked her up in his arms—his neck to keep from falling, or the hem of her skirt. She quickly chose safety over modesty and clamped her hands around his neck as he strode toward the den.

At the couch, he stopped, raised the tip of a boot to a pillow and kicked it to one end. Bending slightly, he laid Malinda down, cushioning her head on the pillow. He promptly stretched out beside her. Propping an elbow on the couch and his cheek against his palm, he rolled to face her. "Ever made out?" he asked.

A high-school term, but Malinda knew well its meaning—knew it, but had never experienced it. She'd wanted this. Heavens! She'd all but asked for it. Yet things were going too fast for her to absorb it all. A button on the couch cut into her back as she inched away from him. "Of course."

Jack chuckled and looped a leg over hers. Catching her by the hip, he hauled her up against him. "You'd make a lousy poker player."

Fighting for time, nervously Malinda licked her lips. "What makes you say that?"

He touched a finger to the corner of her eye. "Your eyes. They talk."

"They do?"

"Yeah." He lifted a hand to her hair and plucked out a pin.

Malinda felt her bun loosen and tensed. Her voice trembled slightly when she asked, "And what do they say?"

"They tell me you've never made out in your life. But that's okay," he was quick to add as he stole another pin. He shook out her hair, then leveled his gaze on hers. "They also tell me you're scared."

All the bravado sagged out of Malinda. It was one thing to be a total innocent, wanting more than anything to feel and experience what other women had. It was quite another to have the man you wanted to experience it with know you were scared witless. But he'd already proved he'd see right through a lie. "I am scared," she admitted reluctantly.

"Why? I wouldn't hurt you for anything in the world."

"Oh, it's not you," she hurried to assure him. "It's Aunt Hattie."

"Aunt Hattie?" he repeated, tucking his chin back to get a better look at her. "I thought she was dead."

"She is. But she did an excellent job of raising a prude. To this day I can still hear her lectures on a lady's proper behavior."

"Like ghostly visits?"

"Sort of. When I'm in a situation where I'm about to deviate from one of Aunt Hattie's rules, I can hear her voice as clearly as if she were standing right next to me. It's unnerving to say the least."

Jack remembered her sudden withdrawal the last time they'd been lying this close. He knew it wasn't fair to remind Malinda of such an obviously embarrassing moment for her—but he had to know. "Did you hear her voice the other day at your house when we were, uh—"

He didn't have to finish the question. Malinda knew exactly to what he referred. "Yes."

It was ridiculous to feel relief, but that's exactly what Jack felt. He'd played the scene over and over in his mind a thousand times, looking for his mistake. And it hadn't been him after all! It had been Aunt Hattie!

He caught Malinda's cheeks between his hands and kissed her hard on the mouth. "Thank you."

"For what?" she asked in surprise.

"For salving my male ego. I thought maybe you didn't like the way I kissed."

The statement was so far from the truth, Malinda almost laughed. It also eased her nerves a bit to know she wasn't the only one dealing with insecurities. "Your kisses are perfect," she said and found the courage to place a hand over his heart. "In fact, I wouldn't be opposed to tasting another one."

To his surprise—and pleasure—she did just that. And it wasn't a quick peck as he'd expected. Her mouth closed over his and slowly sipped away at his breath. Something was different. He couldn't quite put his finger on just what, but something was *definitely* different. And he intended to enjoy every minute of it. Without breaking the kiss, he nestled his head on the pillow next to hers.

The den was dark but for a smattering of light from the hallway beyond. The house, quiet as a tomb. In the silence, silk whispered against cotton, buttons snagged and clicked.

Jack wanted skin against skin.

Working a cautious hand between their bodies, he caught the prim silk bow at her throat and gave it a tug. He stripped it from around her neck and tossed it over his shoulder with a careless disregard for the delicate fabric. His fingers found the first button on her blouse, loosened it, then moved on to the second, never once moving his mouth from hers. In the blink of an eye, he had a lace-covered breast in his hand. He moved a thumb across an already budding nipple and smiled against her lips when he felt her arch against his hand.

"That's right," he murmured before trailing a line of fire down the smooth column of her throat. "Let yourself go," he whispered and warmed her breast with his breath. Hooking a finger over the top edge of lace, he eased it down and closed his mouth over the exposed mound.

At the first gentle tug on her nipple, a surprised gasp escaped Malinda's lips and her toes curled in her shoes. One high heel slipped off her foot and landed on the carpet with a muffled thump. Impatiently she kicked off the other one while she sank her fingers into Jack's hair. Beneath her palms the muscles of his jaw worked as he continued to suckle. Closing her eyes, she gave in to the delicious feelings that spiraled through her body.

He laved one breast then the other before burying his face in the valley between. "Malinda..." he murmured, his voice heavy with a need he was trying hard to suppress.

Lovingly she cradled his head in her hands. She had waited a lifetime for these feelings, for this man. She wanted to tell him so, to share with him what she felt, but the words wouldn't come. So she used her hands. Tugging his shirt from the waist of his jeans, she smoothed her palms up his bare back.

His skin was as smooth as a baby's, but the muscles beneath were all man. At the base of his neck, she touched a finger to a vertebra and traced his spine to his waist. She felt him shudder and marveled at her power to produce it.

With a muffled groan, he rolled, trapping her beneath the weight of his body. Catching the hem of her skirt, he eased it up until his hand met the juncture between her thighs. Again he found silk and lace. So like her. Softness and femininity.

Easing a finger beneath the thin strip of elastic, he stroked. Inches. Bare inches he traced, back and forth, back and forth, but the gentle teasing had Malinda writhing beneath him.

She discovered a need to touch stronger than her need for air. She threaded her fingers through the hair above each ear, then laced them to clasp his head in her hands. She experienced anew his strength, in the corded muscles of his neck, in the crush of his lips against her.

Sensation stacked upon sensation as his fingers moved butterfly soft at the very core of her femininity.

A lady's first and foremost concern is her—

Malinda's body went cadaver stiff beneath Jack's. His fingers stilled. Leaning back, he searched her face in the dim light and saw the guilt in her eyes, the fear. Aunt Hattie. How in the hell was a man supposed to fight a ghost?

He feathered kisses at her brow, the corner of her eyes, the tip of her nose. Each carried a message. *Trust me. I won't hurt you. Let loose and feel.*

Her arms circled his neck and clung. "Oh, Jack, I want—"

"I know. I know," he soothed, his voice like warm velvet against her ear. He whispered meaningless words to her, much like those he'd whisper to the boys in the night when they were awakened by a bad dream.

Malinda felt her resistance melt away at his gentle soothing, degree by slow degree, until there was only need.

Forgetting Aunt Hattie and a lifetime of constraint, for the first time in her life she let herself feel. Hunger built like an animal clawing its way through her insides, struggling to find what she had felt before. Reaching for Jack, she closed her mouth over his.

The shyness was gone. So was her hesitancy. Jack felt the change, the impatience, the demand for more. His fingers found their rhythm again and she arched against his hand, finding the cadence and matching it with her own.

He covered her mouth with his, taking the lead once again, giving passion for passion. He drove his tongue deep into her mouth and, at the same moment, slipped his finger inside her, claiming her virginity.

Digging her fingers into his shoulders, she arched against his hand while ripples of the most exquisite pleasure spiraled through her body. She felt whole, she felt sated...she felt like a woman fully formed.

Taking his cheeks between her hands, she pressed her lips to his. "I love you, Jack," she whispered in the darkness.

The words chilled him to the bone and had the same effect as a cold shower. He'd been afraid of this. Not consciously, maybe, but subconsciously. A woman who'd just experienced her first climax was bound to consider herself in love with the man who'd produced it. Malinda wouldn't be the first, or the last, to confuse passion with love.

That wasn't to say he didn't want to believe her. He just didn't want to be *stupid* enough to believe her. Hoping to set her straight, to give her an out if necessary, he smoothed a hand down her hair. "I know you think you do right now, sweetheart, and that's normal. But your emotions are running pretty high. Tomorrow you may feel differently."

She didn't. The next morning Malinda awoke with a Cheshire cat smile on her face. She wore that smile all day, drawing teasing comments from Cecile and odd looks from her editor at the newspaper and the boys.

No one understood her cheerful mood, the new spring in her step, her all's-right-with-the-world breeziness—with the exception of perhaps Cecile. But Malinda admitted nothing.

She was in love for the first time in her life and the feeling was too wonderful, too special, too new, to share.

That night as she set the dining room table for dinner, adding special touches here and there, she knew what Jack Brannan didn't. Her love had nothing to do with passion and everything to do with the man.

The room alone made Jack uncomfortable. When he'd built the house four years before, Laurel had insisted they needed a formal dining room for entertaining. To his memory, they had used it twice. Once at Christmas. Once for a cocktail party that in his opinion had been a boring flop.

At the moment, the room was being used to let the boys try out their newly learned manners.

A lace cloth covered the table. Since he'd never seen it before, Jack assumed Malinda had brought it from her home. The china was familiar, though, as was the silver. Laurel had always had expensive taste.

He tugged at the tie Malinda had insisted he wear, and reminded himself for the umpteenth time to play along. The torture—or rather, the meal—couldn't last long.

A hand dropped to his shoulder and lightly squeezed. Jack's hands froze on the knot of his tie. He glanced up just as Malinda leaned forward to fill his water glass, her free hand still burning a hole through his shirt. It wasn't the first time that day that she had touched him...although for his part he'd been careful to keep his hands to himself. Her declaration of love had hog-tied and gagged any openness or freedom of expression he'd ever known.

Her hand slipped away and he breathed again as he watched her move to her chair.

"Pass the mashed potatoes."

"Please," Malinda instructed automatically as she scooted her chair closer to the table.

Jack, Jr., rolled his eyes. "*Please* pass the mashed potatoes."

Satisfied, Malinda smiled and passed the bowl. "Darren, we eat with one hand. The other we rest on our lap."

A forkful of roast beef halfway to his mouth, Jack glanced up. She wasn't even looking at Darren. She was busy smoothing her napkin over her lap. He cut his gaze to Darren and watched the boy slide his left hand from the tabletop to his lap. Guiltily Jack did the same.

"Did you finish your homework, David?" she asked as picked up her knife.

"Yeah."

"Yes, ma'am," she corrected, then turned to Darren as she deftly cut a triangle of meat. "How about you?"

Darren was nothing if not quick. He smiled broadly— which was difficult, since Jack had seen him stuff at least half a roll in his mouth just prior to Malinda asking the question—and gave the appropriate response.

A disapproving frown pursed Malinda's lips. "Don't talk with your mouth full, please."

Darren practically swallowed the roll whole. "But you asked me a question!"

"Chew your food properly, swallow, then reply."

Darren heaved a frustrated breath.

Jack looked at the food on his plate, the arsenal of equipment aligned on either side of it and dropped his fork to his plate in disgust. Five minutes ago he'd been starving to death. Now his stomach was tied up in knots.

Napkin on your lap, elbows off the table, please and thank-you, don't talk with your mouth full, sit up straight in your chair. Who in the world could remember all that crap? He looked at Malinda at the opposite end of the table. She was dabbing her napkin at the corners of her mouth like her lips might break.

He wanted to laugh, but didn't dare. He was sure there was some rule he hadn't yet heard that prohibited laughter at the table. She glanced up and caught him staring. A small shy smile curled at her lips. The look was at once seductive and demure.

The heat was instantaneous. He felt it curl in his stomach and spread. Last night he'd taught Malinda a few lessons about herself, how to let loose and feel. In the process he'd learned some things about himself. He'd discovered a patience he hadn't known he possessed, a tenderness that both surprised and pleased him.

In giving, he'd received a more precious gift. Her love. Or at least a declaration of love. And that scared the hell out of him.

He wanted to believe she loved him, but didn't dare. He couldn't forget the differences between them—big differences—and he for one knew how differences could tear a relationship to shreds.

From the moment he'd met her, he'd known he was outclassed. Living with her had only sharpened that knowledge. But he'd seen changes, damn it. She'd learned to open up, first with the boys, and now with him. He'd witnessed a few bursts of anger—all directed at him. But that was okay! Anger was an emotion and he didn't want her to suppress it any more than he wanted her to suppress her desire.

Looking at her, his sons flanking him on both sides, he wanted more than anything to narrow the gap that separated them. And that want went gut deep.

For starters, he'd show her another way to eat. One without the pressure to perform. One without all this damn pomp and ceremony.

Determinedly he picked up his fork and scooped up a spoonful of potatoes. "Good meal, Malinda." He shoveled the potatoes in his mouth, careful to chew and swallow before he added, "But tomorrow night's our turn. The boys and I'll cook dinner while you put up your feet and take a breather."

"That's not necessary. I'm perfectly capable—"

"Sure you are," he assured her expansively. "But just the same, dinner's on us."

Malinda sat in the study, letters from readers stacked neatly at her right. A sheet of typing paper was rolled around the carriage and a bottle of correction fluid stood ready to use.

But Malinda couldn't work. Not one letter of the alphabet marred her page. Her ears strained to catch sounds from the kitchen. They had been in there an hour already. What in the world could they be doing? She caught her lower lip between her teeth and gently gnawed. Granted, it was sweet of them to offer to cook dinner. She certainly could use the time to work on her column. But she couldn't work for worrying. Were they keeping an eye on Patrick? She knew his curious nature. A pot handle turned within his reach was an invitation for him to grab hold and sneak a peek. An image of him being scalded by some unknown boiling liquid made her shudder.

And the twins! They were at that awkward age. All arms, elbows and feet. They couldn't walk across the room without tripping or knocking something to the floor. Especially Darren, she fretted, catching her lower lip between her teeth again.

A loud bang followed by a bloodcurdling scream and Malinda was on her feet. She was halfway across the room when Jack stuck his head in the door. "Nothing to worry about. Darren just dropped a skillet on his foot. Dinner'll be ready in about five minutes, so find a stopping place," he said with a nod toward the desk.

Malinda glanced back over her shoulder to the untouched letters and the glare of white typing paper. "I'm almost done," she lied with what she hoped was a convincing smile and grabbed for the doorknob. "Why don't I give you guys a hand?"

Jack caught the door, refusing to let her out. "No deal. Dinner's on us, remember?" With a smile, he closed the door in her face.

Fuming, Malinda strode across the room and flopped down on the chair, crossing her arms at her breasts. Her foot tapped out a beat that would have a flamenco dancer gasping for breath. She kept up the beat for the full five minutes—or at least until Darren opened the door and announced dinner was ready.

Not knowing what to expect—but fearing the worst—Malinda trailed behind him. When she stepped into the kitchen, her worst nightmare came true. The room was a shambles. Cupboard doors hung open. Drawers gaped wide. The countertops had all but disappeared beneath a jumble of pots and pans and dripping utensils. Smoke hung thick in the air.

Her gaze drifted to the table where paper plates were scattered helter-skelter across a red-and-white checked cloth. In the center of the table a huge platter of french fries gleamed under a film of grease thick enough to cut. Inch-thick hamburgers teetered on a second platter. Jars of mayonnaise, mustard and a gallon jug of ketchup, straight from the refrigerator, finished off the decor.

"Well? What do you think?"

Malinda's gaze flicked up to find all five Brannans standing behind the table, their smiles lip-splitting proud. How was she going to get through this? she wondered fleetingly. She painted on a bright smile. "Great! Absolutely great."

Then Jack was beside her, pulling out a chair. "Your chair, madam," he gushed with a flamboyant wave of his hand. Malinda hadn't sat down before David was waving the platter of fries in her face.

The hamburgers came next. The buns looked as if they had been pounded on with a fist. Malinda gingerly lifted one of the juicy, mutilated mounds from the pile, and in the process bumped her elbow against the ketchup bottle shoved in her direction. Her fingers dripping in grease, she searched for a napkin.

Jack was on his feet in a flash. "Oops. Sorry." He peeled off a long stretch of paper towels from the dispenser by the sink, tore off one and handed it to Malinda. "We like our hamburgers juicy," he said with a wink.

Juicy? Malinda eyed her plate and feared she would need the entire roll of towels to deal with this mess. Smothering a sigh, she reached for her fork. It wasn't there. She ran her hand beside her plate, then lifted it and peered underneath.

"Problem?" Jack asked over a generous bite of burger.

"I was looking for my fork."

"What do you need with a fork? Hamburgers are best dealt with by hand."

Both his circled a bun and he lifted them, demonstrating.

"The french fries," Malinda said with a dubious glance at her plate.

"Use your fingers," Darren suggested and promptly picked up a fry, dredged it through a pool of ketchup and popped it in his mouth.

Malinda swallowed hard as she eyed the greasy potatoes. "Right."

Deciding the hamburger the lesser of two evils, she picked hers up and took a delicate bite. Her eyes bugged open and her taste buds snapped to red alert. Nothing that looked *this* bad could possibly taste *this* good, she told herself. She chewed, swallowed and stole another bite just to be sure.

Jack watched her close her eyes and savor. "Pretty good, huh?"

Malinda flipped open her eyes. "Good?" she garbled over a third bite. "This is delicious."

She wiped her mouth—wiped, Jack noted, no ladylike dab—and dived for the fries.

A man-sized belch rang out. Every hand at the table froze in midmovement. Every head turned to Jack. His eyes widened in innocence. "Wasn't me," he denied with a negative shake of his head.

Another burp and every head turned, this time toward Patrick. He sat propped in his high chair beside Jack. A ketchup-painted smile stretched ear to ear. He tucked his chin to his chest, patted his stomach—an obvious imitation of his father—and said in a deep, childish bass, "Good beer."

For a moment Malinda just stared at him, her mouth gaped wide. Then she laughed. Not a sweet little giggle, but a throw-back-your-head, belly-clutching laugh.

And Jack smiled. Smugly.

* * *

"Malinda, I don't feel so good."

This was the third morning in a row Darren had complained of not feeling well. On the other two—once she'd ascertained there was nothing physically wrong—she'd convinced him to go on to school. "What doesn't feel good?" she asked patiently.

"My tummy."

Malinda bit back a smile as she flipped the last pancake from the griddle to a plate. If Darren's tummy hurt, it was no wonder. The night before he'd eaten four slices of pizza and drunk a gallon of cola. "Maybe you'll feel better after you have your breakfast," she soothed as she guided him to the table.

"I don't think so."

Pancakes were Darren's absolute favorite, which made Malinda take a second look. The child did look a little pale. She pressed a hand to his forehead. Clammy, but not unduly warm.

"When did it start hurting?"

"When I woke up."

"Is it worse now?"

"Uh-huh."

She dropped to one knee in front of him and smoothed the hair back from his face. "Think you better stay home from school today?"

She caught a glimmer of relief in his eyes before he masked it with a soulful look. "Yeah, guess I better."

That little glimmer caused Malinda a moment's concern. She was a firm believer that a child shouldn't miss school unless they were truly sick. A little test might be in order, she decided. "You should go straight to bed and I'll bring you some dry toast and some juice."

When Darren turned his back on the stack of pancakes and shuffled back down the hall, Malinda was convinced. The child had to be sick. Mentally she began to rearrange her day.

She'd just phoned Cecile to get her to cover for her at the shop when Jack walked into the kitchen.

"Good morning," he said, his voice still gruff with sleep.

"Good morning." Without sparing him a glance, Malinda pushed a coffee cup in his hand, then stretched to pull lunch boxes from the cupboard.

Malinda was always a whirlwind of activity in the morning, but usually—or at least for the past couple of days—his appearance in the kitchen usually slowed her down for a minute. Feeling the sting of rejection, Jack propped a hip against the counter and watched her fly past him, wondering what in the world was behind this rush of activity.

"Darren's sick."

So, that's it, he thought and relaxed a little.

"Nothing serious," she added as she picked up a knife and started spreading peanut butter on bread slices laid out. "Just a tummy ache." She deftly wrapped the sandwich in plastic wrap, dropped it in a lunch box, then picked up the knife again. "I don't think we need to call the pediatrician. He doesn't seem to be running a fev—"

Jack plucked the knife from her hand and dropped it to the counter before spinning her around to face him. Dropping his hands to her waist, he dipped his head to meet her gaze. "And how is Malinda?"

He read her much too well. She dropped her forehead against his chest. "Frazzled. I have a thousand things to do today and I'm not sure Darren's really sick." She lifted her head and looped her arms at his waist. The gesture was as natural and easy as the smile she offered him. "This is the third morning in a row he's complained of not feeling well.

Something tells me he simply doesn't want to go to school. Any suggestions?" she asked hopefully.

Jack bussed her a quick kiss. "Yeah. I'll stay home and you go do your thousand things."

Chuckling, Malinda shook her head. "No. That's all right. My day is easier to rearrange than yours. And besides, I've already called Cecile to cover for me." She pushed out of his arms. "Now scoot or I won't finish the lunches and the boys will be forced to eat yucky cafeteria food."

Jack shrugged into his jacket as he strode for the back door. "I'm going to run by your house and check on the plumber. He's supposed to finish up today. I'll call later and check on Darren."

Before the door closed behind him, Malinda called out, "Oh, Jack!"

He stuck his head back in the doorway. "What?"

"Don't forget tonight is open house at the children's school."

He frowned. "I have a zoning meeting at six." When he saw the disappointed look on her face, he added, "Don't worry. I'll meet you there."

Nine

———

Parents circled the classroom, talking in low whispers, admiring their children's work displayed on the wall. Malinda milled among them, nodding and smiling to a few familiar faces in between taking dainty sips of punch provided by the PTA. No one, but no one, would have guessed that beneath the demure smile and ladylike facade lay a boiling rage. But it was there. Boy, was it there!

She'd already visited Jack, Jr.'s, and David's classrooms. She'd sat in miniature chairs, calmly thumbed through folders filled with art and admired Jack, Jr.'s, working volcano. When her turn had arrived, she'd visited with their teachers and found both women to be kind and complimentary in their comments concerning the boys' progress over the past month.

And in that Malinda took great pride. But it hadn't reduced the rage. It had been building all day.

Easing her way through the crowded room she approached Darren's teacher. "Mrs. Gordon?"

"Yes," the woman replied, turning.

Malinda immediately knew why Darren and his friends referred to her as "the bulldog." Kindergarten teachers were supposed to be red cheeked, enthusiastic and full of smiles. This woman was anything but. Her skin was sallow and hung off her cheekbones like a limp rag. Her mouth was pulled down in a dissatisfied frown.

Malinda shifted her glass of punch to her left hand and extended her right. "I'm Malinda Compton, Darren's baby-sitter."

Mrs. Gordon ignored the hand. "Yes," she replied, looking down her hawklike nose at Malinda. "I'd heard there was a new one."

The note of disdain in her reply was hard to ignore. But to her credit, Malinda tried. "I understand you and Darren had a problem in the cafeteria last week."

"*Darren* had a problem in the cafeteria," Mrs. Gordon was quick to amend.

Malinda took a deep, calming breath while the rage boiled higher. "Yes, he told me he accidentally spilled his milk."

An eyebrow arched. It did nothing to improve the woman's looks. "I can see he has you fooled." She gave the sleeves of her dress a smart snap. "Fortunately I'm not as easily duped. Perhaps this time the boy's learned his lesson."

Malinda sucked in an enraged breath. "Do you honestly think that by pouring the remainder of his milk over his head you taught him a lesson?" Before Mrs. Gordon could reply, Malinda rushed on. "I can assure you, you didn't. You only succeeded in embarrassing him in front of his friends, so much so that he doesn't ever want to come to school again."

"A little temper tantrum. Children use them often to get their way."

The temptation was too great. Malinda lifted the glass and poured. The red, pulpy liquid streamed down Mrs. Gordon's face.

A collective gasp of horror went up from the parents standing near the two as they jumped back to avoid being splattered by the red punch. Every eye turned to the front of the room.

Malinda set the glass down on the desk and dusted off her hands. She leveled a look on the woman lethal enough to kill as she shoved her purse strap to her shoulder. "How does it feel, Mrs. Gordon, to be made a fool of in front of your peers?" Saying that, she turned on her heel and marched to the door, her chin held high. When she caught sight of Jack lounging in the doorway, his shoulder slouched against the frame, a smile bigger than Texas blooming across his face, she nearly lost her step.

Catching herself, she raised her chin a notch and marched right past him. "Don't say a word," she warned under her breath. "Not one word."

Jack pulled away from the door frame and followed her, chuckling. "I wouldn't dream of it."

He trailed her to the parking lot and her car. She tried to put her key in the door lock, but her hands were shaking so hard she couldn't make the silly thing fit. In frustration, she wheeled to face Jack. "Do you know what that woman did to Darren?"

"Yes. I heard."

"She poured a carton of milk on his head in front of all his friends." Malinda paced to the rear of her car and back.

"That's why he complained of a tummy ache. That's why he didn't want to go to school."

"I know."

She paced to the hood of the car and back, nearly mowing Jack down. He was getting dizzy just watching her. He hopped up on the hood of her car and watched her agitated pacing from a safe distance. "She's cruel and mean and sour and—" Suddenly she stopped, Jack's response finally registering. "How did you know what happened?"

"When I called to check on Darren today he told me."

She dropped her face to her hands. "I can't believe I poured punch over her head."

Reaction had finally set in. For a woman with Malinda's quiet nature, Jack was surprised she'd held it off this long. He caught her hands in his and tugged until she stood between his thighs. In the glow of the parking lot's security light, he caught the angry flush on her cheeks and the shimmer of tears in her eyes. "You were mad."

"Of course I was mad," she said impatiently. "She hurt Darren's feelings, but I've only made things worse. Darren won't *ever* want to go back to school now."

"Oh, I think he will."

"How can you be so sure?"

"I paid a visit to the school principal today and asked Darren to be transferred to another class."

"You did?"

"Yep. Should have done it months ago. The woman's had it in for him since the first day of school."

Remembering again the scene she'd made, Malinda dipped her head against his chest. "Why didn't you stop me?"

"And miss all the fun?"

Her head came up with a snap. "Fun!"

Laughing, Jack folded her into his arms. "You were wonderful. Like a lioness protecting her cub. I loved it." He tipped up her chin until her eyes rested on his. "You are one hell of a woman."

Jack stood at the study window, staring, his hands shoved deep in his pockets. The sun was shining. First time in days. Behind him, invoices and bills of lading were scattered across his desk. A ton of work awaited him, but his attention was stolen by the scene outside.

Across the lawn, Malinda and his sons knelt alongside the fence bordering his property. In deference to Oklahoma's sporadic weather, they were all dressed in sweat suits and lightweight jackets. Even Malinda.

Jack, Jr., held some odd-shaped shovel and was digging holes faster than a gopher. Darren and David crawled behind him, dropping bulbs in the freshly turned earth. Seeing his sons working in the yard was enough to make him stop and take notice, but it was Malinda and Patrick who held him at the window.

Obviously the job of covering up the holes had fallen to the two. Just as obvious was the fact Patrick didn't quite understand his job description. While Malinda would painstakingly smooth the dirt over a bulb and move on to the next one, behind her, Patrick would scoop the clods of dirt right back out.

Laughter rumbling low in his chest, Jack watched this scene for several minutes before Malinda glanced over her shoulder to check on Patrick's progress. When she saw him sitting on the ground, dribbling dirt through grubby fingers, bulbs scattered at his feet, her mouth formed a surprised O. Making a wild grab for the boy, she tumped him to the ground and started tickling. Within seconds all four boys and Malinda were rolling on the grass in a wild tangle of arms and legs. Jack could hear their laughter and squeals through the paned glass.

A stab of regret pierced his heart at the scene. His sons. The changes had occurred so slowly he hadn't even been aware they'd taken place. The sad part was he had been so consumed in daily survival he hadn't even been aware a change was needed. But he could see the boys were more relaxed now. Less rebellious. Patrick had all but quit sucking his thumb. Darren and David weren't troubled with nightmares any longer. Jack, Jr., was smiling more and taking part in family activities, not holed up in his room.

He'd attributed their behavior over the past year and a half to the fact they'd lost their mother. He'd thought in time they'd adjust. Partly that was true. But Malinda was a factor, too. She'd filled a hole in their lives he hadn't been able to fill. She'd touched them where he couldn't.

Sighing, he braced his forearm against the windowpane and dropped his forehead to rest on his arm as he continued to watch. And the boys weren't the only ones who'd changed. Malinda had gone through quite a metamorphosis herself. The sweats alone were proof of that.

Living with her over the past weeks was like watching a flower bloom with the advantage of time-lapse photography. When he'd first met her, she'd been like a rosebud, petals tightly closed, fragile and beautiful in this metamorphic state, but hiding a greater beauty, her true self, within. Over the weeks, with the slow unfolding of each petal, he'd discovered new facets of her personality, qualities she'd suppressed over the years either by design or intent.

A month ago she wouldn't have dared roll in the grass with the boys. She would've never permitted herself the luxury of such uninhibited fun. And she'd never have been caught dead dressed in a man's sweats with holes in the knees and dirt caked beneath her nails.

As he watched, the boys, still laughing, turned back to their work. The wrestling match was over. Jack dropped his arm from the window and stretched, knowing he had to do the same. His arms froze above his head when he saw Malinda stagger and grope for the fence. Her smile was gone, her face a deathly pale. Slowly her knees buckled and she crumpled, like a kite that had lost its wind.

Jack was running before she hit the ground. Jack, Jr., met him at the back door, his breathing ragged, his eyes wide in fear. "Malinda fell. She—"

"I know." Jack brushed past his son, his gaze locked on Malinda's limp form. "Call 911."

Then he was beside her, kneeling in the freshly turned dirt. Smoothing her hair from her face, he took her hand in his and searched for a pulse.

"Is she dead?"

Jack heard the fear in David's voice. It matched the one twisting in his gut. Before he could reply, the scream of the ambulance's siren rent the air. Darren and David, standing at Malinda's head, stepped closer together and caught each other's hand. Patrick let out a sobbing wail.

Still clutching Malinda's hand in his, Jack pulled Patrick to his side. "She's going to be okay, Son. I promise." And prayed like hell he could make good that promise.

"This is absolutely ridiculous," Malinda complained to Cecile as her friend flitted about the room, plumping pillows and closing drapes. "I'm not sick."

"Of course you're not," Cecile agreed patiently. "You're just exhausted, which is exactly what the doctor diagnosed."

Malinda threw a leg over the side of the bed. "Fine. Then I'll go to bed early tonight and get a good night's sleep."

Before she could stand, Cecile was pushing her back down against the pillows. "Oh, no, you don't. The doctor said complete bed rest for two days and that's exactly what you're going to get."

The leg swung right back over the side. "I don't have time to go to bed. Who'll look after the children?"

"The boys are going home with me." At a soft tap on the door, Cecile gave Malinda a shove and called, "Come on in."

Jack poked his head around the door. "Problem?"

Cecile blew a frustrated breath at her bangs. "Yes. Maybe you can do something with her. I give up."

Seeing the stormy look of defiance on Malinda's face, Jack chuckled and stepped into the room. "I can handle things here. The boys are waiting in your car, packed and ready to go."

"Good." Cecile snatched her mink jacket from the chair and shrugged it on. She turned and narrowed an eye at Malinda. "And you stay in bed." Her expression softened and she bent to plant a kiss on Malinda's forehead. "Take care of yourself. I love you."

Alligator tears welled in Malinda's eyes as the door closed behind Cecile. She sniffed and dragged a hand beneath her nose.

Jack noted the unladylike gesture and smothered a smile. Holding out a pill in one hand and a glass of water in the other, he said, "Here take this."

Malinda waved it away.

"Doctor's orders," he reminded her sternly.

"It'll just make me sleep," she complained.

"That's the general idea."

The tears escaped her eyes and rolled down her cheeks. "But I don't have time to sleep. I've got my column to finish—"

"I'll call the paper and tell them to run an old one."

"The laundry is stacked a mile high—"

"Believe it or not, I can wash and fold clothes."

A sob racked her shoulders. "But that's what you pay me to do," she wailed hysterically.

Jack could stand anything but a woman's tears. They made him feel about as useless as tits on a boar hog. He dropped down on the bed and patted her awkwardly on the back. "Don't cry, Malinda. It's going to be okay. You just need some rest, that's all. You've been working too hard. And that's partly our fault. I'm going to hire someone to help with the housework—"

"I don't need help," she cried, then hiccuped. "I just need to get better organized."

Organized, hell! The woman was more organized now than the United States Army. The only way she could accomplish more work was if she were able to somehow split herself in two. But he could see that reasoning with her was getting nowhere fast. He could also see she was overtired and fighting sleep. The boys were the same way at times and the only thing that worked when they were this keyed up was to physically hold them down until they gave up the ghost.

"Whatever you say," he amended readily. He nudged her over with his hip and draped an arm around her shoulders as he lay down beside her. "Try to get some rest now."

Malinda awoke to a gentle snoring in her ear. The room was shrouded in late-afternoon shadows. Jack's room. She wondered a moment why she was there. Then she remembered. Fainting in the garden, coming to in Jack's room with ambulance attendants hovering over her. A house call from Jack's personal physician. The fear. The embarrassment. She shuddered at the memory.

She looked at the bedside clock and was shocked to discover she'd slept the day away. Glancing at Jack, she realized he had, too. And he'd needed the rest as much as she. Turning carefully in his arms so as not to wake him, she touched a fingertip to the dark circles under his eyes, then moved to the worry lines that, even in sleep, plowed between his brows. He worked too hard, slept too little, carried way too many burdens, though he'd rather die than admit it. A wistful smile pulled at her lips.

She loved him. And he was wrong if he thought her naive enough to confuse passion and love. She loved him with all her heart, all her soul. She loved him more than life itself. And she loved his sons, too. All four of them. And she wanted more than anything to convince him of that.

As she watched, his eyes fluttered open, then closed again. Tightening his arms around her, he snuggled her to his chest. "Thought you were sleeping," he murmured.

"I was." She'd hoped for a moment, when he'd hugged her up against him, that he was going to make love to her, but when his eyes remained closed and his breathing took on the rhythmic evenness of sleep, she sighed deeply. Disappointed and somewhat bored, she pressed a fingertip to the bold design on his sweatshirt and slowly began to trace. Up and down, arcing over loops and curves, her finger moved until she'd completed the pattern. Still he didn't budge. Frustrated, she dragged her finger to his waist. She felt a glimmer of hope when his stomach muscles tightened beneath her hand.

He dipped his chin and peered at her through the slit of one eye. "What are you doing?"

She glanced up, her expression innocent. "Nothing."

Frowning slightly, he caught her hand and pulled it back to his chest, then dropped his head back against the pillow. Though his eyes remained closed, Jack was now wide-awake...and painfully aware of every curve of the body molded against his side.

When he'd first carried her into the house after her fainting spell, she'd been as dirty as a mud-slinging two-year-old. But at some point—probably while he'd been helping the boys pack—she'd changed from the grungy sweats and had taken a bath. He hadn't noticed the change earlier when he'd taken over from Cecile. He'd been too concerned for Malinda's welfare, too intent on getting her to rest. But now scents filled his head, as sweet and flowery as the thin cotton nightgown that V'd dangerously low at her breasts.

Cool it, Brannan, he warned himself. *She's half-sick, dead tired and way too vulnerable.*

He'd almost convinced himself he could resist temptation when her fingers started moving again on his shirt. Heat crawled up his chest.

"Malinda?"

"Hmm?" she said distractedly.

"Don't do that, sweetheart."

"Don't do what?"

He lifted his head to peer at her again. This time through both eyes. The look she gave him back was hot, languid and wanting. Slowly she lifted her face to his.

"Make love to me, Jack," she whispered against his mouth.

He attempted to back away. "I can't."

Malinda inched closer. "Can't or won't?"

Jack had posed that same question to her once in an attempt to get her to own up to her real feelings. Now the shoe was on the other foot. And it was squeezing like hell. "Doesn't matter whether I can't or won't," he argued gently. "It's you—I'm thinking of you. You're sick."

She draped her upper body across his chest and smiled a wicked smile. "Do I look sick?" she asked, arching one eyebrow coyly.

Jack knew exactly how Dr. Frankenstein must have felt. By encouraging Malinda not to suppress her emotions, he had created one hell of a monster. His gaze traveled to her breasts where her hand fluttered at a tiny silk bow. Below it, he saw a shadowed cleavage, and a flash of bared flesh. He jerked his eyes back to her face. "N-no," he stammered, fighting for control. "You don't look sick. But you're weak," he insisted. "The doctor said you should stay in bed."

"I am in bed."

"Now, Malinda—" he reasoned patiently.

"Now, Jack," she mimicked, then laughed. Leaning closer, she kissed him full on the mouth. "I guess I'll just have to make love to you, then." Her fingers found the hem of his sweatshirt and tugged it up.

Jack tugged it right back down. "Malin—"

She smothered his stern warning with her mouth as she scooted to her knees and levered herself above him, pressing him deeper into the feather pillows.

Her arms circled his neck and her fingers settled on muscles stretched tighter than the elastic on Aunt Hattie's best girdle. "You're tense," she scolded gently as she pushed back to sit on his thighs. She tapped a manicured nail against her cheek and eyed him thoughtfully. "Tension comes from suppression. I wonder what you could be suppressing?"

The question was sincere enough, but the mischievous glint in her eye and the teasing tone of her voice gave her away. He *had* created a monster, he decided. Or at the very least, a witch or a vamp. And he wasn't one damn bit sorry.

Hooking his knees at her side, he flipped her to her back. then he was looming over her, a hand pressed on either side of her head. "I'll show you what I'm suppressing," he threatened in a husky voice. "And what I've been suppressing for days."

If he'd thought to frighten her, he failed miserably. Malinda laughed gaily and threw her arms around his neck, pulling him to her.

He showed her what he'd been suppressing. With his hands, with his lips. And he told her. Whispered words, passionate promises, that warmed parts of her body his hands couldn't touch.

He took her on a journey only lovers know. Down paths strewn with soft, fragrant petals. Up steep hills that left her gasping for breath. Rides on fluffy clouds, suspended above the world, and rocketing down snow-covered slopes, her breath stolen by the wind. She experienced it all wrapped in the warmth and security of his arms.

When she thought she had seen everything, tasted all of love's pleasures, he braced himself above her, his own breath coming in deep, grabbing gulps. With his gaze leveled on hers, he buried himself deep inside her. Her head fell back, her eyes closed, as together they reached journey's end. Paradise.

He watched the emotions wash across her face, listened as she whispered his name. And he knew without a doubt this woman was made for him. Call it destiny. Call it fate. Whatever tag placed on their meeting, he knew it was meant to be. "I love you, Malinda," he whispered.

And she loved him, she thought as she gazed deeply into his eyes... but she couldn't resist teasing him just a little. "I know you think you do right now," she quoted, trying to imitate his deep bass voice. "And that's normal. But your emotions are running pretty high. Tomorrow you may feel differently.''

Jack stared at her, his mouth slightly agape as he listened to his own words played back to him. Then he tossed back his head and laughed at the ceiling. Catching her to him, he rolled until she was on top. ''Well, we'll just have to see what tomorrow brings, then, won't we?''

Tomorrow brought sunshine and lazy smiles. Without the boys to care for, Malinda and Jack had the house to themselves.

Determined Malinda would follow the doctor's advice, Jack kept her in bed until nearly noon. It was a hardship, he conceded good-naturedly as he snuggled next to her naked body, but somebody had to do it.

To look at her was to love her, but Jack's feelings rooted much deeper than that. In Malinda he found a soul mate, someone who shared his dreams, his views on family and life. They still had their differences, but instead of seeing them as an obstacle, he now saw them as a bonus. Their very differences made them an even stronger team and Jack viewed marriage and family as a teamwork effort.

He passed the morning watching her sleep and daydreaming about their future, a life centered around her and his sons. She'd make a hell of a mother. She'd proved that over the weeks. She'd also make one hell of a wife.

He knew his plans were selfish, that they should be making them together, but he wasn't quite sure he should share them with her just yet.

There were things to do. Parts of his life he had to get in order before he approached Malinda with a new proposition, one which offered a deeper commitment, more permanence than their current arrangement. He wanted to give her everything, all the things she'd missed out on as a child, and in order to do that he needed first to get his own life in order.

Hunger finally drove him to the kitchen where he whipped together peanut-butter-and-jelly sandwiches and served them to her in bed on a silver tray, making Malinda laugh. They spent the afternoon nestled in pillows, munching microwave popcorn and sipping soft drinks, while Jack entertained her with video tapes of the boys as babies.

It was Malinda's first encounter with Laurel, Jack's wife and the boys' mother. And though she would have preferred it otherwise, she had to admit the woman was beautiful. Her hair was the color of sunshine, her eyes a rich, creamy brown. Though the boys resembled their father most, she could definitely see characteristics they'd inherited from their mother. Especially the twins.

She felt odd, lying there next to Jack and watching a part of his life he'd shared with another woman. Not that he hadn't spoken of his past. He had. But there was something about watching it all that made her feel like a trespasser.

Even on film Malinda saw evidence of the life Jack had portrayed. The progress was obvious—from their teeny first home with its hodgepodge furniture, to the last film taken in the house they now lived. Every birth, birthday and Christmas celebrated in vivid color. Jack, Jr., as a chubby baby, babbling and splashing while his mother struggled to bathe him. The twins perched in their high chairs, each with a cake on his tray bearing a single lit candle, and a bevy of voices singing "Happy Birthday" in the background. Patrick, no bigger than a doll, napping on his daddy's chest.

Though Laurel appeared throughout the tapes, Malinda had the oddest sensation the woman hadn't really been there at all. There was something about her—in her eyes, maybe, or in her nervous movements—that made her appear as if she were looking for a means of escape. In a sense, perhaps she had.

Jack had shared with Malinda Laurel's unrest, her constant search for happiness. In Malinda's eyes, all the ingredients had been right there in front of her. A home with four healthy children and a husband who obviously adored her. Who could ask for more?

When the television screen turned to snow and the sound an ocean's roar, Jack climbed out of bed to turn off the video recorder. "Hard to believe they're the same boys, they've changed so much."

His wistful comment touched Malinda's heart. She stretched out a hand and he took it as he sat down beside her. She snuggled next to him. "In size, perhaps, but they're basically the same."

"Now, maybe." Jack sighed and lay back against the pillows, pulling Malinda with him. His fingers massaged her scalp. "The boys suffered a lot after Laurel's death. And I wasn't much help. I was going through a pretty tough time myself." His fingers locked on her head and he slowly swiveled his hand, turning her to face him. "You've pulled them through. I thank you for that."

Embarrassed by his praise, Malinda diverted her eyes. "I didn't do anything."

"Yes, you did. You loved them and believed in them."

"They're easy to love."

The comment was so ridiculous Jack had to laugh. "Easy to love? Malinda, get real. The boys did everything in their power to make you hate them."

"Their pranks were only a cry for love and attention."

"Well, trust me when I tell you they had five baby-sitters prior to your coming to live with us, and not one of them ever considered the boys' pranks a plea for love and attention.''

Malinda stood outside the school auditorium surrounded by what she had grown to think of as her brood. With a nervous glance at her watch, she looked toward the double doors that led to the parking lot outside.

"He's not coming."

The flat statement came from Jack, Jr., and mirrored Malinda's own thoughts. But she couldn't let Jack, Jr., know that. She had to offer him hope. She stooped to adjust his tie. "Sure he is," she said, forcing a confident note in her voice. "You know how the airlines are. His plane's probably late. He'll make it. You'll see." She straightened and gathered Patrick's hand in hers. "I guess we better find our seats."

Malinda sat through the program, her attention divided between the performance taking place on stage and the auditorium's rear door. Patrick sat on her lap, the twins to her right. On her left was an empty seat.

Mr. Humphrey, the school's principal, moved to the microphone. "Jack Brannan, a student in Mrs. Perkins's fourth-grade class, will recite the *Gettysburg Address.*"

Pride filled Malinda's chest as she watched Jack, Jr., approach the microphone center stage. Dressed in a light blue oxford shirt and navy cotton slacks, his hair carefully parted and combed, he looked like a little man. A miniature version of his father. He stood tall and proud as he spoke into the microphone.

"Four score and seven years ago our fathers brought forth on this continent . . ."

His voice, pitched deep, filled the auditorium. Tears brimmed in Malinda's eyes, blurring her vision. They'd worked hard for two weeks, memorizing and rehearsing Lincoln's famous speech. And he was doing so well!

"...the unfinished work which they who fought here have thus far so nobly advanced."

His eyes traversed the auditorium as he spoke, just as Malinda had coached. He never once stumbled or hesitated...until his gaze found Malinda and his brothers and settled on the empty seat beside her.

She saw the disappointment in his eyes, in the slight tremble of his lips. But the hesitation only lasted a split second—though to Malinda it felt like a year—before he lifted his chin valiantly and finished.

"—and that government of the people, by the people, for the people, shall not perish from the earth."

Moved by the impassioned speech, everyone in the auditorium rose to their feet and applauded. Malinda dabbed her eyes. She stood Patrick in the empty seat next to her and rose, too, clapping until her hands stung.

Unfortunately the audience's congratulations for a job well done wasn't enough. She saw that in the tight set of Jack, Jr.'s, mouth before he turned his back on the crowd and returned to his seat at the rear of the stage.

The one man whose approval he'd needed most hadn't been there to give it. That knowledge tore at Malinda's heart.

Malinda ducked inside the car and unhooked the straps from Patrick's car seat while the boys waited impatiently on the driveway.

"Don't look at me," Jack, Jr., warned in a threatening voice.

"I wasn't lookin' at you. I was lookin' at the moon."

"Sure you were, nerd," he said sarcastically.

Malinda sighed deeply. Three steps forward, ten back. "Boys, that's enough," she said patiently as she pulled a sleepy-eyed Patrick from his seat.

Just as she straightened, Jack wheeled his Blazer onto the driveway behind her car, blinding her with his headlights. He jumped out and strode toward them, his face creased by a broad smile. "Hey, guys! How was the program?"

Jack, Jr., turned his back on his father and headed toward the house. "Whadda you care," he mumbled.

Jack frowned as he watched the back door slam behind his oldest son. "What was *that* all about?"

"I'll explain later," Malinda said quietly. She shifted Patrick in her arms. "Why don't you help the twins into their pajamas while I put Patrick to bed."

Putting Patrick down for the night was easy as the child was exhausted, but Malinda remained in his room, silently moving about, her mind as well as her heart in turmoil as she put away toys and clothes.

Jack, Jr., hadn't been the only one to feel the squeeze of disappointment at his father's absence. She had, as well. But her heart went out to the boy. As a young girl, she'd experienced that same pang of disappointment when her parents had missed important events in her life. How many times had she scanned a crowd, looking for her parents' faces, knowing they weren't there but wishing with all her heart they would be?

Aunt Hattie had been there, though. She'd never missed one of Malinda's school programs. But somehow it had never been the same. Just as Malinda's presence hadn't been enough for Jack, Jr. He'd needed his dad.

The problem as Malinda saw it was her. Her presence in the Brannan household had freed Jack to get even more involved in his business. With her there to care for the boys and take them where they needed to go, Jack was able to travel more, work later hours and pursue more contracts.

She had to leave. That was obvious. But it didn't mean she wanted to. As she tucked the blanket to Patrick's chin, tears filled her eyes and her heart ached until she thought it would surely break. She loved the Brannan boys. Almost as much as she loved their father. And she loved them enough to give them back to one another.

She turned from Patrick's bed and sniffed back her tears. Raising her chin in determination, she went in search of Jack.

She found him in the kitchen, pouring coffee into two mugs.

"Patrick asleep?" He handed her one of the mugs, then pulled out a kitchen chair, gesturing for her to sit down.

"Yes. He was so tired I think he was asleep before his head hit the pillow."

Jack chuckled. "The twins, too." He stirred in sugar, then took a cautious sip. Sighing his pleasure at the kick of caffeine, he reared his chair back to two legs. "Well, how was the program?"

"Wonderful. Jack, Jr., did a great job."

"Knew he would. The kid's a winner."

Malinda remembered the look of disappointment on Jack, Jr.'s, face when he'd seen the empty chair. "Yes, he is. But he was also very disappointed his father wasn't there to share in his success."

Jack dropped his chair to all four legs and molded his hands to his mug. "My meeting in Chicago ran long and I had to take a later flight. I figured you could handle things here."

The last bit of hope she'd clung to sagged out of Malinda. She'd wanted the reason for Jack's absence to be something out of his control. A delayed flight, a flat tire.

Anything but a conscious decision to miss his son's program.

Fighting to hide the tremble in her lips, Malinda pursed her mouth. "It doesn't matter now, anyway. The program is over." She took a deep breath and plunged on. "The painter called today while you were out of town and said he'd be finished with my house by the weekend. He's already completed the upstairs and all that remains is the kitchen ceiling."

The sudden switch in conversation took Jack totally by surprise. The arctic blast with which it was delivered made him more than a little nervous. "What are you saying?"

"That I'll be moving home Friday. That was our arrangement, remember?"

"Yeah, I remember, but I took it for granted you'd—"

"Perhaps you've taken too much for granted."

Her words were like a slap in the face. Betrayal and abandonment—the same sensations he'd felt when Laurel had left the last time—turned his heart to stone. Jack shoved back his chair from the table, the look on his face thunderous. "I guess maybe I have," he said and strode angrily from the room.

Ten

"**K**ind of quiet without Patrick around, isn't it?"

Malinda refused to take the bait. Cecile had been casting for weeks, trying in her not-so-subtle way to get Malinda to talk, but Malinda refused. The wounds were still too fresh.

"Since there aren't any customers at the moment," Malinda said, ignoring Cecile, "I think I'll vacuum."

The invoices hit the counter with a frustrated slap. "For pity's sake, Malinda. You've got to talk about—"

Malinda switched on the machine and drowned out Cecile's voice.

No, I don't have to talk about it, she told herself as she shoved the heavy machine back and forth across the plush carpet. *Not yet, anyway.* She had to heal first. Heal enough so that every time she thought about Jack and the boys, she didn't cry.

And if Cecile thinks the shop is quiet, Malinda reflected as she broadsided a wall with the vacuum, *she should live in Aunt Hattie's house for a while!* In comparison, the shop was an amusement park—bright lights, people, noise, laughter. She'd never realized how painful silence could be, how lonely. Until now.

Life with the Brannans had spoiled her. Her days with them had been filled from dawn until dusk with a frenzy of activity, laughter and riotous noise. Now she rattled around her house, alone, living out her life as Cecile had always predicted—as that of an old maid.

A hand reached around her and shut off the machine. Malinda jumped, then frowned when she turned to find Cecile standing behind her.

Still looking miffed, Cecile thrust a handful of envelopes at her. "Your mail," she said, then added sarcastically, "Or are you going to give up that form of communication, as well?"

Guiltily Malinda accepted the envelopes. "No, I'm still accepting mail."

Cecile spun on her heel. "Maybe I should consider writing you a letter, then," she tossed back over her shoulder.

Malinda's soft voice stopped her before she'd taken three steps. "I'm sorry."

Cecile wheeled back around, her offended look dissolving the instant she saw Malinda's grief-stricken expression. Gathering her friend into her arms, she gently rocked her to and fro. She'd spent the better part of her life trying to protect Malinda from all the bumps and scrapes in life. She'd assumed that protective role at the age of ten and never once looked back. In her opinion, of the two of them, Malinda was the fragile one, the one with the big heart, the one most susceptible to pain.

In her role as protector, Cecile had received probably as many black eyes as she'd given. As she felt Malinda's tears mix with her own on her cheek, she knew if giving Jack Brannan a black eye would mend Malinda's heart, she'd gladly deliver the punch. But she didn't think that was the answer. In her eyes, Jack had proved himself the day Malinda had fainted. He'd stepped in and taken over, fussing over Malinda like an old mother hen. On that day, Cecile had handed over the reins. Jack loved Malinda and she loved him. Cecile could see that. She just wished they'd both quit being so stubborn and admit it.

Sniffing, she backed from Malinda's embrace and shook a finger under her friend's nose. "Don't you think I've forgiven you yet, because I haven't." She sniffed again and stole the tissue Malinda had just retrieved from her pocket to dab at her eyes. Stretching to her full height of an unintimidating five foot two, she folded her arms at her waist. "We're sisters, remember? We pricked our fingers and mixed our blood when we were ten years old and swore to share all our secrets. Not once since then have you ever refused to confide in me."

"I know."

"Then why can't you talk to me now?" Cecile cried impatiently.

Fresh tears brimmed in Malinda's eyes. "Because it hurts."

Her reply tore at Cecile's heart. She caught Malinda's hands in hers and squeezed. "Sure it does, honey, but you need to talk about it. Don't bottle it all up inside."

Malinda's lip quivered uncontrollably. "I miss them," she said . . . and the dam finally broke.

Cecile guided the sobbing Malinda to the bench. "I know you do," she murmured sympathetically.

Balancing the envelopes on her lap, Malinda dug in her skirt's pocket for another tissue. "I worry about them so much," she cried as she twisted the tissue around her fingers. "You see, Patrick has this rash that springs up occasionally, and if you don't put cream on it right away it spreads. And Jack, Jr.," she said on a hiccupy sob. "He's smart as a whip, but he requires an enormous amount of encouragement and attention to keep him on the right course." She dragged the tissue beneath her nose. "The twins pretty much look out for each other, but they need guidance, you know?" She lifted her face to Cecile, her eyes swimming in tears.

The information told Cecile everything and nothing. Everything about Malinda's feelings for the boys, but absolutely nothing about her feelings for their father. Patience was not Cecile's long suit. She believed in getting to the core of the problem without wasting time. But considering Malinda's present state, she knew understanding was the key. Cecile patted her knee consolingly. "Yes, I know, but don't you think their dad is meeting those needs?"

"Jack?" Malinda blew out a disbelieving breath. "Financially, yes. Emotionally..." She paused, her brows knitting together in a frown. She shook her head as she plucked an envelope from her lap. "I don't know," she said helplessly. "He loves them. I do know that. And he spends time with them. But he has this ridiculous notion he has to work constantly in order to provide them their every whim." Her gaze settled on the letter's return address and she grimaced when she saw it was from the Collection Bureau of America.

Ripping the envelope open, she said in an irritated voice, "You know, these people have probably spent more in postage, sending me late notices, then the total of my debt."

Her eyes quickly scanned the brief message, then widened in disbelief. "I can't believe this!" she said, gasping.

"What?"

Malinda waved the letter beneath Cecile's nose. "This!" she cried and pulled the letter back to scan the page again. "There must be some mistake," she murmured as she read. "It says here my debt's been paid in full."

Cecile strained to read over her shoulder. "Your parents, maybe?"

Malinda vehemently shook her head. "No. They aren't even aware of the collection agency's involvement."

Giving up, Cecile bent to retrieve the torn envelope from the floor, hoping for a clue. "Then who?"

Both women raised their heads at the same moment and stared at each other, their eyes wide. "Jack," they whispered simultaneously.

Malinda leaped to her feet, dumping the remaining envelopes to the floor. She paced three steps and whirled. "But why?"

Cecile slowly rose to her feet, watching Malinda carefully. "I don't know."

"Well, I won't let him."

"No, you shouldn't," she agreed, but cheered silently, *Way to go, Jack!*

"He thinks he can throw money on a problem and make it disappear." Malinda's lips thinned and her hands found their way to her hips. "But this time it won't work. By golly, I'll tell him a thing or two."

Cecile hid her delight behind a mask of righteous indignation that mirrored her friend's. "That's right, Malinda," she said as she headed for the coat rack, dragging Malinda behind her. "You tell that Jack Brannan he can't treat you this way." She shoved Malinda's arms in the coat's sleeves and snugged the collar to her chin. Spinning her friend toward the door, she grabbed Malinda's purse from the desk and thrust it into her hands. "You march over to his office right now and tell him you won't accept his charity."

Without giving Malinda a chance to change her mind, Cecile pushed her out the door and pulled it shut behind her. Laughing, she collapsed against the door.

She couldn't have concocted a better way to push Jack and Malinda together if she'd schemed for a week.

Jack dropped his pencil and punched the intercom button, irritated by the interruption. "Yes?"

"There's someone here to see you," Liz informed him.

It was the third time that afternoon Jack's concentration had been broken by a salesman. "Tell him I'm busy."

Liz's voice came back through the speaker. "I think you'll want to see this one."

The note of mystery in her voice had Jack rolling his eyes in disgust. "I told you I don't want to be disturbed. Make an appointment for later this week."

Frowning, he picked up the pencil again and, using the eraser end, started punching figures into his calculator. When the office door opened, he didn't even glance up. "Liz, I told you I don't want to be disturbed."

A letter fluttered to his desk, covering up the column of figures he was totaling. Without looking at it, he shoved it aside. "You must not value your life, otherwise you wouldn't keep bugging me."

"I pay my own debts."

Jack slowly raised his head. Malinda, not his secretary, stood opposite him, her chin held high, her cheeks stained an angry red. She'd never looked more beautiful or more alluring. He wanted to hate her for that.

He reared back in his chair, tapping his pencil against his opposite hand, his face a closed mask. "I'm sure you do," he agreed. "But I owed you for the care you gave my sons."

"We made an agreement. I'd serve as your housekeeper and baby-sitter and you'd take care of the repairs on my house with no money exchanged between either party."

"True," he said and leveled his chair. "But in my opinion the scales were tipped in our favor. You gave a lot more than you received."

"That's right. I *gave,*" she said, her emphasis on the last word. "And it's impolite to try and pay for a gift."

Jack searched for patience. "Malinda, I'm only trying to help. I assure you, I won't miss the money."

"I'm sure you won't. But as I said, I pay my own debts."

"Then consider it a loan."

"Fine." Malinda whipped out her checkbook and propped it on the desk. Flipping it open, she felt her courage wane slightly when she caught sight of her bank balance. Ignoring the paltry amount, she wrote out a check just short of it, knowing full well she'd be eating peanut-butter sandwiches for the remainder of the month. "My first installment," she said and tossed the check to the desk.

Jack looked at it but didn't pick it up. "I don't want your money."

"And I don't want your pity *or* your charity." Having had her say, Malinda spun on her heel and headed for the door.

"Malinda?"

Her hand on the doorknob, she stopped but didn't look back. "What?"

"The boys miss you."

Her shoulders drooped. As usual, he wasn't playing fair. "I miss them, too," she whispered. *And you.* She twisted

open the door and strode out before she shamed herself
with tears.

Cecile greeted Malinda at the entrance to the shop wearing an expectant smile. "Well? How did it go?"

"Fine." Malinda passed her by.

"Did you get the money business straightened out?"
Cecile persisted as she followed in hot pursuit.

"Yes. We agreed to call it a loan and I gave him a check
for my first installment."

Cecile's step faltered and her mouth fell open. She hurried to catch up. "But I thought once you saw each other,
you'd—"

Malinda wheeled to face her friend, primed for a fight.
"We'd what, Cecile? Kiss and make up?" The anger
quickly peeked, then waned. Cecile didn't deserve this ver-
bal attack. Malinda was mad at Jack. And herself, she admitted ruefully as she shrugged out of her coat, for being
such a fool. She shook her head as she draped her coat on
the rack. "No," she said. "He merely felt a sense of obligation to me. By paying off my debt, he thought to free
himself of any sense of duty."

Everything was there, ready for his final approval. Contracts, power of attorney, new signature cards from the
bank for his business account, letters of explanation and
introduction to all the companies he was currently under
contract with. The attorneys had been thorough. All Jack
had to do was sign on the dotted line. Twice he put his pen
to paper. Twice he withdrew it without leaving a mark.
Frowning, he reared back in his chair, propping his elbows
on the armrests and his chin on his hands.

He'd searched for weeks for the right man for the job and
finally found him. Like Jack, Collin Ryan had learned the

building business from the ground up. He was a hard worker, as honest as the day was long and knew when to cut a bad deal loose.

All Jack had to do to seal their business arrangement was to put his name on the dotted line. In doing so, he'd relinquish control of his out-of-state contracts and reduce his travel time to a manageable amount. But suddenly it all seemed useless.

He'd done it all for Malinda. And now she was gone.

"Like hell," he mumbled as he jerked his chair upright. Dropping his hand to the paper, he signed his name on the dotted line. Jack Brannan had gone up against tougher obstacles than Malinda Compton and won. By damn, he would this time, too.

The intercom, buzzed, interrupting his thoughts.

"Yes, Liz."

"Jack," she said, her voice harried, "Mrs. Dunlap is on the phone. She said it's an emergency. The boys have—"

Without waiting to hear the rest of the message, Jack punched the blinking red light, disconnecting his secretary. "What's wrong, Mrs. Dunlap?"

"It's the boys," his housekeeper cried hysterically. "They've run away. I've looked everywhere, but I can't find them."

Fear had him gripping the receiver tighter in his hand. The boys had pulled a lot of pranks over the past two years, but they had never run away. He shoved back his chair, sending it spinning crazily into the wall. "I'll be right there," he said before slamming down the receiver.

Tight-fisted buds clung to the trees lining the street in front of the shop. Here and there sprigs of green peeked through the narrow strip of yellow-brown grass that stretched between the sidewalk and the parking lot. Pansies, their delicate petals open and smiling, filled the neighboring bank's triangular-shaped garden. Malinda loved all the color, from the deep velvety purples to the butter-soft yellows.

Ordinarily the showy display would draw a smile from her. Not today.

As she headed for her car, her head bent, her shoulders drooping disconsolately, she pushed on sunglasses in deference to the sun's late-afternoon glare. The days were growing longer now. Another sign spring was in the air.

But Malinda couldn't have cared less. She was preoccupied, her thoughts centered on her meeting with Jack, as she drove home. She hadn't permitted herself to dwell on his appearance at the time—she couldn't or she would have lost her edge. But she hadn't missed the tension lines on his forehead or the dark circles beneath his eyes. He wasn't taking care of himself.

She sighed as she turned her car onto her street, knowing she wasn't weathering the separation much better than he. Food was out of the question, sleep something she succumbed to only out of exhaustion. With a negligent glance toward the front of the house, Malinda angled onto the driveway. Stomping on the brakes, she snapped her head back around. Huddled on her front porch's top step were Jack, Jr., David and Darren. Patrick played at their feet.

Her fingers cinched tight around the steering wheel, she closed her eyes, sure she was dreaming, then looked again. They were still there. Patrick dropped the roly-poly he was playing with and waved.

Malinda swung open her door and hurried across the lawn. The boys met her halfway. Dropping to her knees, she gathered them into her arms, laughing and talking at the same time.

"How did you get here?" she asked as she strained to see if perhaps she'd missed Jack's Blazer at the curb.

Darren's chest swelled in pride. "We walked. Jack, Jr., showed us the way."

Malinda thought of the four miles that separated the two houses and all the cross streets in between. She shuddered and hugged Patrick tighter to her chest.

"Not that I'm not thrilled to see you guys, but why are you here?"

"We ran away."

Malinda's mouth dropped open. "Ran away? But why?"

"Mrs. Dunlap said she was going to send us to a juvenile home."

Enraged, Malinda lurched to her feet. "She *what?*"

Taking up the tale, Jack, Jr., said, "Yeah, she said we were juvenile delinquents and belonged behind bars."

David looked up at Malinda, his eyes full of fear. "Please don't let them send us to jail."

Gathering the boys protectively to her sides, Malinda herded them toward the house. "Nobody is going to send you to jail, sweetheart," she soothed.

After parking the boys at her kitchen table, Malinda threw together sandwiches and stirred up a fresh pitcher of lemonade. The boys attacked them as if they hadn't eaten in a week.

Ignoring the napkin Malinda had placed by his plate, David swiped the back of his hand across his mouth. "This is sure better than gruel. Mrs. Dunlap says that's all they serve behind bars."

If possible, Malinda's fury fired a little higher. Jerking the receiver from the kitchen wall unit, she punched in Jack's office number. After three rings, she heard the answering machine click on.

"The office of Brannan Construction is closed for the day. Please leave your name, number and the time of your call after the tone. Thank you."

Beep.

"Jack, this is Malinda." She glanced at her watch. "It's six-fifteen. I have the boys and I'll—"

Beep.

Frustrated, she depressed the plunger and quickly punched in the Brannans' home number. The phone rang and rang. Malinda stifled a groan as she slammed down the phone. Now what?

Turning to the boys, she said, "Hurry and finish your sandwiches, fellows. I've got to take you home."

Darren scooted as close to Malinda as the seat belt would allow. "Do you think Dad's gonna be mad at us?"

Malinda smiled down at the boy to ease his fear. "Maybe a little."

"Do you think he's gonna punish us?"

"Probably. But only because he loves you," she was quick to add. "Running away from home is a pretty serious offense." She stopped at a red light and turned to look at the boys. "It's also not the answer to a problem. Your daddy loves you very much and he'd never let anyone take you away from him, no matter what you hear to the contrary. Is that clear?"

Three heads nodded. When Patrick, who was strapped in a seat belt with Jack, Jr., saw his brothers' action, he bobbed his head, too.

Silence weighed heavy in the car the rest of the trip. But when Malinda pulled to a stop in front of their home, she heard a mumbled, "Uh-oh," from the back seat. She turned her head and saw Jack standing on the front porch, his arms folded across his chest. His stern expression was enough to make Malinda want to gun the car down the driveway and take the boys back to the safety of her house. But that wouldn't do. They were guilty and must suffer the consequences of their actions.

The boys slowly climbed from the car and lined up along its length, their heads bowed. Obviously unaware of his father's anger and the predicament they were all in, Patrick bolted for the porch and wrapped his arms around his dad's legs.

It only took a split second for Jack to melt. He scooped Patrick up and hugged him tight against his chest. Cupping the boy's head in the palm of one broad hand, he tucked it beneath his chin. Malinda watched his Adam's apple bob convulsively.

She blinked back her own tears.

Drawing a shuddery breath, Jack said, "Boys, you have some explaining to do. Wait for me in the den." He settled Patrick to his feet and pushed open the door and waited while they filed by. His expression once again stern, he turned to Malinda. "I'd appreciate it if you'd sit in on this discussion."

She backed toward her car. "That's probably not a good idea. This is a family matter."

"The boys involved you when they ran away to your house."

When she continued to hesitate, he added, "Please."

Her hand on the car's door handle, Malinda inwardly groaned. She didn't want to stay. She wanted to go home. Seeing him again was simply too painful. But the "please" got her. Reluctantly she followed him to the den where the boys waited on the couch.

"Okay, boys. Let's hear it. Jack, Jr.," he said, leveling a stern look on his oldest son. "You begin."

"Well—" Jack, Jr., swallowed hard and glanced from his father to his brothers, then back again. "Mrs. Dunlap said she was going to send us to a home for juvenile delinquents, so while she was cooking dinner we snuck out the front door."

Jack dipped his chin, narrowing an eye at his son. "Mrs. Dunlap said that?"

"Well-l-l...something like that."

"Just exactly what did she say."

Jack, Jr., hung his head. "She said if we didn't change our ways we were going to end up in a home for juvenile delinquents."

"Which is not quite the same as saying she was going to send you there, is it?"

"No, sir."

"So why did you make up this wild tale?"

"We thought if Lindy thought Mrs. Dunlap was being mean to us, she might come back and live with us again."

Malinda's mouth fell open. Jack shot her a glance, then looked back at his sons.

"What you did was wrong. You scared the wits out of Mrs. Dunlap. You lied to Malinda. You endangered your and your brothers' lives by running away. What do you have to say for yourselves?"

"We're sorry, Dad," Jack, Jr., mumbled.

"Yeah, we're sorry," the twins repeated.

"Sorry isn't going to cut it. You'll have to be punished." Jack heaved a frustrated breath. "Go to your rooms and get ready for bed. We'll finish this discussion in the morning."

They filed out, past their father and Malinda, their heads hanging low. As Darren passed by, he peeked up at Malinda. His sorrowful look tugged at an already straining heart. He stopped in front of her and dipped his head. "I'm sorry we lied to you, Lindy. We didn't mean any harm."

Her heart lodged tight in her throat, Malinda knelt and took his hands in hers. "I know, sweetheart." Unable to say more, she ruffled his hair, then tipped up his chin and offered him a smile.

"Would you give us our baths?" he asked.

Malinda glanced up at Jack.

"It's okay with me." He turned his back and headed for the kitchen. "I'm going to call Mrs. Dunlap. She's worried sick," he added over his shoulder.

Malinda survived the bathtime ritual. Barely. She even survived supervising—again at the boys' insistence—the cleaning of their rooms. But when they begged her to read them a bedtime story, Malinda nearly lost her carefully controlled emotions. Of all the stories available, they had to choose *Sleeping Beauty*.

As a child, the story had always been Malinda's favorite. She'd often dreamed of being awakened by a prince's kiss and living happily ever after in a castle with the man she loved. Unfortunately, as an adult, she'd thought she'd found her prince in Jack Brannan. His kiss had definitely brought her to life. He'd awakened feelings in her lying dormant for too many years.

Malinda shook herself and forced herself to read the last line. "And they lived happily ever after." She closed the book and set it down.

"One more story, Lindy. Please? Just one," David asked in his most beseeching voice.

"That's it for the night, boys," Jack ordered from the doorway.

While Malinda tucked Patrick in, Jack herded the older boys to their rooms. When they bumped into each other in the hallway after leaving the boys' rooms, the atmosphere was suddenly tense.

Twisting her hands at her waist, Malinda smiled weakly. "I don't think they meant to scare you."

"No. They usually don't."

Her smile slowly dissolved as she glanced back toward the boys' rooms. Oh, how she was going to miss them!

Sensing that her role in this drama was over, her presence no longer needed, Malinda collected her purse when she reached the den. "I guess I better head home."

"I'd like to talk to you for a minute."

Malinda froze midstep, yanked to a stop by the entreaty in Jack's voice. Every nerve ending in her body screamed for her to keep walking, out the front door and out of their lives before they completely broke her heart. Without looking back—she didn't dare for fear she'd throw herself into his arms—she said, "I'm sorry for whatever part I played in the boys' rebellion."

"That's what I'd like to talk to you about."

His voice was closer now. Almost directly behind her. A hand touched her shoulder, confirming his proximity, and though his touch was gentle, it nearly sent her through the floor. Fortifying herself, she squared her shoulders and turned beneath his hand.

Before she could utter a word, he said softly, "They miss you, Malinda." He tucked a stray wisp of hair behind her ear, then dropped his hand to her shoulder. He dipped his head to meet her gaze. "And they want you to come back home."

Home? The enticement was there, but Malinda steeled herself against the temptation. Being the boys' baby-sitter was simply too painful. And it wasn't enough. She wanted more. She started to speak and he placed a finger to her lips, silencing her. "Please hear me out." He placed a hand to the small of her back. Guiding her toward the couch, he said, "To set the record straight, Mrs. Dunlap is a really nice lady. She isn't the type to play mind-warp games with the boys. Unfortunately they've been hellions ever since you left."

He dropped down next to her and immediately slumped until his shoulders were nearly even with hers. He cocked his head to look at her and gave her one of his hard-to-resist grins. "As usual, they blamed me for your leaving."

Lacing her fingers together on her lap, she stared at them. "I'm sorry. They shouldn't have done that."

"No need to be sorry. I figured they were probably right." Cupping his hands behind his head, he crossed his boots at the ankles and relaxed.

Malinda was anything but. Their bodies now touched at the shoulder, elbow and thigh. Nervously she wet her lips.

"The problem is," he continued. "I don't know what I did this time to make you leave."

"You didn't do anything to me. It was the boys. With me around to cover for you, you were spending more and more time away from home. Missing Jack, Jr.'s, school program was a perfect example. I thought if I were gone, you'd be forced to take a more active role in their lives."

Jack dropped his head to the back of the couch and chuckled. "I can't believe this."

"Believe what?" she asked in puzzlement.

He rolled his head to look at her. "I can't believe you left because I didn't come to the program."

Furious that he looked upon the incident so casually, Malinda sawed her skirt to her knees and in the process put a good two inches between her and Jack. He closed the gap right back up. Twisting her head around to glare at him, she said, "You should have been there."

"You were there," he replied calmly.

"But he needed *you*," she flashed back.

"No." Jack dropped his hand to her lap and captured her fingers in his. "He needed both of us." Lifting his gaze to hers, he looked long into her eyes. They were still the sweetest blue he'd ever seen, but there was a trace of confusion there he hoped to dismiss. "Did you ever wonder why I was late that night?"

"I didn't have to wonder. You told me your meeting ran long."

"Right. But weren't you curious as to why I was having such long meetings in Chicago?"

"No, business is business to my way of thinking."

"True, but not a totally accurate picture." He lifted an index finger and toyed with the edge of her nail. It was a playful, almost distracted action, but electricity shot up Malinda's arm. "I stayed late in Chicago so I'd hopefully never have to miss another one of the boys' school programs." The nail poised on the ball of his thumb, he glanced up. "I did that for you as well as the boys."

"Me?" Malinda echoed in surprise.

"Yeah, you. But more precisely, for us."

"Us?"

"The boys learned a lot from you in the short time you were with us. But you taught me something, too. A very important something. I had the mistaken impression that the boys needed *things* as much as they needed me. I was killing myself trying to provide it all when what they needed most was me. Since you've been gone, I've realized they need you in their lives, as well. What I'm trying to say is, will you consider living with us again?"

"Living with you!" Malinda was on her feet and across the room before Jack could stop her. Her arms squeezed tight around her waist, she stood at the den window, her gaze fixed on the scene outside, her back to him.

Jack could tell by her defensive stance he had blown it. Malinda had totally misconstrued what he was trying to tell her. But then who could blame her? He never had been any good with pretty words. He was tempted to slip into the boys' rooms and ask for some advice. They certainly knew how to charm her.

Pushing off the couch, he crossed to her and placed a tentative hand at her shoulder. "Malinda?"

Impatiently she shrugged his hand off her shoulder. "What?"

"I think you misunderstood what I was saying."

"No, I think I understood perfectly. You want me to move back in as your housekeeper and baby-sitter."

"I had in mind a more permanent arrangement."

Malinda tensed, but willed herself not to read anything into the statement.

He placed his hand on her shoulder again and slowly turned her to face him. "I don't want you as a house-keeper or a baby-sitter. I hired Mrs. Dunlap to fill those duties." He gathered her hands in his. "And I hired a man in Chicago. Collin Ryan. All the long meetings were with him and a handful of attorneys, working out the legal and financial arrangements. In the future, he'll be taking care of all the out-of-state contracts. I'll still have to travel some, but for the most part I'll be home every night. I want a family, Malinda," he said, squeezing her hands in his, willing her to believe him. "It's what I've always wanted."

He took a deep breath, searching for just the right words to let her know his heart. Only the simplest came to mind. "I love you, Malinda. I want you to be my wife and a mother to my sons. I want you to share our home, our lives."

Her dream. A home, a family. The happy ending she'd always wanted but dared not hope for. Her lips trembling uncontrollably, Malinda jerked her hands from his and flung them around his neck.

Caught off guard, Jack fought for balance, laughing as he asked, "Is that a yes?"

Tipping back her head, Malinda looked up at him, smiling through her tears. "Only if you say 'please.'"

The swinging door that separated the den and the kitchen swung open and all four boys tumbled out. "Say it, Dad!" Darren begged, clamoring to his feet. "Just say it!"

Laughing, Jack caught Malinda in his arms and pulled her flush up against him. Looking deep into her eyes, he murmured, "Please," before closing his mouth over hers.

*   *   *   *   *

This is the season of giving, and Silhouette proudly offers you its sixth annual Christmas collection.

SILHOUETTE

Christmas Stories

1991

Experience the joys of a holiday romance and treasure these heartwarming stories by four award-winning Silhouette authors:

Phyllis Halldorson—"A Memorable Noel"
Peggy Webb—"I Heard the Rabbits Singing"
Naomi Horton—"Dreaming of Angels"
Heather Graham Pozzessere—"The Christmas Bride"

Discover this yuletide celebration—sit back and enjoy Silhouette's Christmas gift of love.

SILHOUETTE CHRISTMAS STORIES 1991 is available in December at your favorite retail outlet, or order your copy now by sending your name, address, zip or postal code, along with a check or money order for $4.99 (please do not send cash), plus 75¢ postage and handling ($1.00 in Canada), payable to Silhouette Books, to:

In the U.S.	**In Canada**
3010 Walden Ave.	P.O. Box 609
P.O. Box 1396	Fort Erie, Ontario
Buffalo, NY 14269-1396	L2A 5X3

Please specify book title with your order.
Canadian residents add applicable federal and provincial taxes.

SX91-2

Angels Everywhere!

Everything's turning up angels at Silhouette. In November, Ann Williams's ANGEL ON MY SHOULDER (IM #408, $3.29) features a heroine who's absolutely heavenly—and we mean that literally! Her name is Cassandra, and once she comes down to earth, her whole picture of life—and love—undergoes a pretty radical change.

Then, in December, it's time for ANGEL FOR HIRE (D #680, $2.79) from Justine Davis. This time it's hero Michael Justice who brings a touch of out-of-this-world magic to the story. Talk about a match made in heaven . . . !

Look for both these spectacular stories wherever you buy books. But look soon—because they're going to be flying off the shelves as if they had wings!

If you can't find these books where you shop, you can order them direct from Silhouette Books by sending your name, address, zip or postal code, along with a check or money order for $3.29 (ANGEL ON MY SHOULDER IM #408), and $2.79 (ANGEL FOR HIRE D #680), for each book ordered (please do not send cash), plus 75¢ postage and handling ($1.00 in Canada), payable to Silhouette Reader Service to:

In the U.S.
3010 Walden Ave.
P.O. Box 1396
Buffalo, NY 14269-1396

In Canada
P.O. Box 609
Fort Erie, Ontario
L2A 5X3

Please specify book title with your order.
Canadian residents add applicable federal and provincial taxes.

ANGEL

Take 4 bestselling love stories FREE

Plus get a FREE surprise gift!

Special Limited-time Offer

Mail to Silhouette Reader Service™

In the U.S.	In Canada
3010 Walden Avenue	P.O. Box 609
P.O. Box 1867	Fort Erie, Ontario
Buffalo, N.Y. 14269-1867	L2A 5X3

YES! Please send me 4 free Silhouette Desire® novels and my free surprise gift. Then send me 6 brand-new novels every month, which I will receive months before they appear in bookstores. Bill me at the low price of $2.49* each—a savings of 30¢ apiece off cover prices. There are no shipping, handling or other hidden costs. I understand that accepting the books and gift places me under no obligation ever to buy any books. I can always return a shipment and cancel at any time. Even if I never buy another book from Silhouette, the 4 free books and the surprise gift are mine to keep forever.

*Offer slightly different in Canada—$2.49 per book plus 69¢ per shipment for delivery. Canadian residents add applicable federal and provincial sales tax. Sales tax applicable in N.Y.

225 BPA ADMA   326 BPA ADMP

Name _____ (PLEASE PRINT)

Address _____ Apt. No. _____

City _____ State/Prov. _____ Zip/Postal Code _____

This offer is limited to one order per household and not valid to present Silhouette Desire® subscribers. Terms and prices are subject to change.

DES-91   © 1990 Harlequin Enterprises Limited

'TWAS THE NIGHT
Lass Small

Happy Holidays!

We invite you to spend Christmas with the wonderful Brown family. In this special holiday package you'll meet Bob Brown, who is reluctantly cast opposite Josephine Malone in a seasonal classic. But as the two rehearse, practice begins to make perfect—romance.

And don't miss *The Molly Q,* the first book about the Brown family. To order *The Molly Q* (#655) send your name, address, zip or postal code, along with a check or money order (please do not send cash) for $2.75 plus 75¢ postage and handling ($1.00 in Canada), payable to Silhouette Reader Service to:

In the U.S.	In Canada
3010 Walden Ave.	P.O. Box 609
P.O. Box 1396	Fort Erie, Ontario
Buffalo, NY 14269-1396	L2A 5X3

Please specify book title(s) with your order.
Canadian residents add applicable federal and provincial taxes.   SDNIGHT-R